D0205519

Stolen Child

Marsha Forchuk Skrypuch

Scholastic Canada Ltd.
Toronto New York London Auckland Sydney
Mexico City New Delhi Hong Kong Buenos Aires

Scholastic Canada Ltd.
604 King Street West, Toronto, Ontario M5V 1E1, Canada

Scholastic Inc.
557 Broadway, New York, NY 10012, USA

Scholastic Australia Pty Limited
PO Box 579, Gosford, NSW 2250, Australia

Scholastic New Zealand Limited
Private Bag 94407, Botany, Manukau 2163, New Zealand

Scholastic Children's Books
Euston House, 24 Eversholt Street, London NW1 1DB, UK

Library and Archives Canada Cataloguing in Publication

Skrypuch, Marsha Forchuk, 1954-
Stolen child / Marsha Forchuk Skrypuch.

ISBN 978-0-545-98612-0

I. Title.

PS8587.K79S86 2009   jC813'.54   C2009-905493-0

ISBN-10 0-545-98612-5

Cover photo courtesy of Lauren Shear.
Cover: torn paper detail © iStockphoto.com/sx70.

6 5 4 3 2 1   Printed in Canada   116   10 11 12 13 14

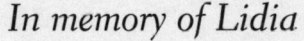

In memory of Lidia

Contents

Chapter One

1950 – Coming to Canada

The woman who said she was my mother was so ill on the ship from Europe that she wore a sickness bag around her neck almost the whole time. The man I called father had come over a year before us. He had worked in different places in Canada, looking for one that could be our home. He wrote to us that he'd settled on Brantford, Ontario, because of the trees and the two Ukrainian churches. And a foundry that gave him a job — which meant that we could eat.

Because Marusia was so sick on the ship, she spent most of her time down below. I do not like to feel closed in, so I let her sleep in peace. I was left with lots of time on my own, and I didn't mind. I would run up the stairs to the top deck and lean over the railing, watching the water churn far, far below me. Once, I climbed over the railing and sat on the edge, dangling my legs over the open water and relishing the cool clean air. I was there less than a minute when a deckhand snatched me by the waist and lifted me to safety. He yelled at me in a language that wasn't Ukrainian or Yiddish or German or Russian. It wasn't English either. I suppose he told me that I was crazy to be doing such a thing. It didn't feel crazy. I was finally alone and out in the open, if only for a moment. It felt like freedom.

When the ship landed at the Port of Halifax, I followed Marusia down the gangplank. I had gotten so used to the rolling of the sea that when my feet touched Canadian soil, I thought it was moving. I had to hold onto a post to stop from falling. Marusia was unsteady on her feet too. She was carrying the suitcase and couldn't reach the post, so I grabbed her hand and steadied her, then we walked to the end of the long, snaking line of immigrants.

At the front of the line stood men in uniform, who interviewed every newcomer. That scared me speechless. What would they ask me about? What could I say?

Marusia squeezed my hand reassuringly. "Remember to call me Mama."

When it was our turn, the officer looked at our documents, then bent down until he was eye level with me. His craggy face was kind, but the uniform terrified me. He said in Ukrainian, "Welcome to Canada, Nadia. Are you glad to be here?"

I don't like to lie, so I didn't answer, but just stared at him through my tears. I was glad to finally be out of that terrible Displaced Persons' camp we had been in for five years. In some ways, I was glad to be in Canada because it was so far away from my other life. But there were things about my earlier life that I still yearned for.

The immigration officer tugged on one of my pigtails

and then stood up. I listened as he asked Marusia questions about where we came from before the war, and what we did during it. I always noticed how easily Marusia lied.

The officer asked to see the train tickets that the United Nations people had given us. Marusia held them up, not wanting to let them go, but he snatched them from her and examined them carefully. Only when he seemed satisfied did he stamp our papers and hand the tickets and our papers back. Marusia folded them with trembling hands and shoved them through the buttons of her carefully ironed blouse and into her bra. The man gave her some paper money. "That's five Canadian dollars. For food," he said.

The port was thick with other people who had lost their homelands in the war, just like us. Vendors competed with each other, trying to sell us food. They shouted things like "milk," "apples" and "bread." Marusia had tried to learn some English in the DP camp, and so had I, so we could understand some of the words.

Marusia wanted to buy meat sandwiches and a bottle of milk, but she didn't know the word for sandwich. When she finally got a vendor to understand her, he wanted too much money. We needed to be careful so our money would last. I was hungry and thirsty and thought I would die of heat. But at least we were safe.

"I think that is a food store," I said, pointing to a building with a pyramid of tin cans displayed in the window. The door of the building opened and a man walked out. He carried what looked like a loaf of bread.

"Let us try," said Marusia, pushing me towards the store.

When we opened the door, it was even hotter inside than outside. A rosy-faced man with a barrel belly and a shiny hairless head grinned at us.

"Food . . . ?" said Marusia in English, holding the five-dollar bill up for the man to see.

"Not much left," said the man in English, gesturing with his hands to help us understand.

We looked around the store. He was right. The cans arranged in a pyramid had pictures of different vegetables on them. There were sacks of flour and rice. But no buns or cheeses or sausage or anything that could be eaten without preparation.

"Bread?" asked Marusia.

The storekeeper shook his head sadly.

We were about to leave when the man's face brightened. He crooked his finger and we followed him to the back corner of the store. As he opened up a giant box, a *whoosh* of lovely icy air enveloped us. He pulled out what looked like a large white cardboard brick. "Ice cream," he said, grinning.

"I scream?" Marusia asked, puzzled.

"No, no," the man said.

I was as confused as Marusia. What did this screaming thing have to do with bread?

The man grabbed the cardboard brick and took it to the front counter. He frowned in concentration as he shuffled through a box under his cash register. Smiling, he held up two flat wooden spoons. "Now you'll see," he said, peeling back a paper layer from the cold brick. A vanilla scent swirled towards us.

"Ice," said the man. Then, "Cream." He took one of the

wooden spoons and dragged it across the surface of the brick. A cold ball formed. He poised it on the spoon and held it to my mouth. "Taste," he said.

I clamped my mouth shut.

"I will try," said Marusia in her careful English. The man held the spoon to her opened mouth and dropped in the cold ball as if he were feeding a bird. Her eyes widened with shock. I was so glad that I hadn't tried it first. But then she grinned. "Good!" she said.

She rolled a bit onto the other spoon and gave it to me. I touched the strange food with the tip of my tongue. It reminded me of a snowball. I put the entire spoonful into my mouth and shivered at the shock of cold creamy sweetness. It wasn't just the wonderful taste, but the sensation of cold on a hot sticky day. It was heavenly.

"Five dollars," said the storekeeper.

Marusia blanched. A whole five dollars for this strange new food? She shook her head.

"You eat; you buy," he said sternly.

Marusia reluctantly held up our five-dollar bill. "But this is all we have."

The shopkeeper grabbed it from her fingers.

"Please," she said, tears welling up in her eyes.

The shopkeeper gave us a pitying stare. He reached into his till and took out a one-dollar bill. Marusia took it.

We walked out of the store, Marusia clutching our precious ice cream to her chest. We were barely halfway down the block when she cried, "Oh no. Look!"

Her blouse was covered with thick white liquid. "Hold this," she said, shoving the container into my hands. She reached through her buttons to her bra and took out our precious immigration papers and our train tickets. A corner of one form was wet and a portion of the official stamp was now illegible. The train tickets were damp but not damaged. She waved them in the air, drying them. Meanwhile I stood there, watching our four-dollars' worth of ice cream melt in the heat. She gingerly re-folded the immigration papers and train tickets and shoved them beneath the waistband of her skirt.

"Let us sit there," she said, clutching my elbow to direct me over to a park bench. The minute we sat down she handed me a wooden spoon. We slurped the ice cream as quickly as we could. By the time we were finished, our hands and faces were sticky, but I didn't care. That ice cream was the best thing I had tasted in a very long time. We cleaned ourselves off at a public fountain, but Marusia's blouse no longer looked freshly ironed.

I don't remember all that happened over the next few days. We managed to find our way to the train station. I knew we were travelling west and I remember switching trains in Quebec City. We stopped long enough in Montreal to find a food store. We only had that one-dollar bill. The ice cream had been such a costly treat!

One of the other immigrants travelling on the train suggested that we buy something called Wonder Bread. "It's cheap," she said. "You could buy three loaves with your dollar."

So we went into a grocery store and asked the red-lipsticked cashier where we would find Wonder Bread. "Down the aisle," she said in a bored voice, pointing with a long red fingernail. An entire shelf was filled with fluffy white loaves wrapped in colourful waxed paper. Marusia took two. We didn't dare buy anything to drink, and besides, there was a water fountain outside. The cashier gave us several coins in change.

When we got back onto the train, Marusia opened up one of the bread packages and drew out a couple of slices for each of us. It looked like perfect white bread, with a soft golden crust. I held it to my face and breathed in. It had no smell. I took a bite. It had no taste. I looked at Marusia. She was chewing slowly, with a puzzled expression on her face. "I wonder why they call this bread," she asked. Then she chuckled sadly. "Wonder Bread."

I felt like crying. Would this be the only kind of bread we could eat in Canada?

Marusia patted my hand. "I'll bake some real bread when we get to our new home."

With the motion of the train, and my hunger staved off with Wonder Bread, I drifted off to sleep, dreaming of real bread.

Our train chugged through Ottawa, then we switched trains in Toronto. I was amazed that Marusia could keep it all straight, but each time the train stopped, she would show our tickets to the conductor to make sure we were going in the right direction. These trains were enclosed, with soft chairs and big windows — nothing like the flatcars in Germany. I stared out the window as the cities flashed by, surprised that there were no bombed-out buildings, no burnt-down cities. Had the war not travelled across the ocean? I guess it was not a world war after all.

By the time the train pulled into Brantford, we had eaten the two loaves of Wonder Bread and I was truly sick of it. At the Brantford train station, I could see Ivan — the man I am supposed to call Father — waiting outside the station for us. His face was freshly shaved and his hair was combed back and still wet. His hands were shoved deep into the pockets of a carefully pressed pair of worn grey pants.

When we stepped off the train, his face broke into a grin. We were just steps away from the train when he wrapped his arms around Marusia and gave her a loud kiss — right in front of everyone.

I tried to pretend I didn't know them, but then he caught me up in his arms and hugged me close. I tried to push him away, but he held on tight. "You are safe, Nadia," he whispered. "We will not let anyone harm you ever again."

I would not hug him back, but instead went limp. I didn't want more of a scene.

Ivan grabbed Marusia's battered old suitcase and put it in the trunk of his big black car. I had no luggage — my few items of clothing had fit easily into Marusia's suitcase. We got into the car, just as if we were a real family. I had not been in a car for a very long time. I settled into the back seat, enveloped in the scent of leather and gasoline . . .

A large black car driven by a man in uniform . . . .

"Nadia, open your window a little and let the breeze cool you," Marusia said. Then, turning back to Ivan in the front, "Did you buy this car, Ivashko?"

"No," he replied. "It belongs to my boss. He loaned it to me today so you could have a grand arrival to our new home."

Marusia's eyes crinkled with pleasure and she brushed her husband's cheek with her fingertips. "That was so very thoughtful of him," she said. "It reminds me of when we got married."

I remembered that too. They got married in the DP camp. Not right inside the camp, but in a little Austrian church outside it. The Austrian priest let a Ukrainian priest from the camp do the service. Afterwards, we had all taken a taxi back to the camp. That car had been small and old, the leather seats cracked with age.

I settled down for a long ride, but within minutes Ivan turned down a street of mostly older looking brick houses. I noticed some smaller wooden houses built in between. He pulled up in front of one of these. It looked like it had just been built.

"You bought a house, Ivashko?" Marusia asked with surprise.

"I bought some land, Marusia," he answered. "I am building a house."

Marusia and Ivan got out of the car but I stayed sitting in the back seat. What was the matter with me? All this time, I had wanted the journey to be over. Yearning to be home. But was this really my home?

Ivan opened the back door of the car and held out his hand to me. "Nadia," he said. "I made a swing for you in the backyard."

Twelve-year-olds are too old for swings, I know that, but I smiled anyway. It was the thought that counted: Ivan tried so hard. I stepped out of the car. Ivan retrieved Marusia's suitcase from the trunk and the three of us walked to the front door.

Ivan opened the door and set the suitcase inside. He turned to Marusia with a grin on his face, picked her up as if she were a child and carried her through the door. "What are you doing?" she cried. "Put me down!"

"It is a Canadian custom," said Ivan. "It is supposed to bring good luck."

He set her down on the floor just inside and I followed them in, thankful that he didn't carry me over the threshold as well.

On the outside the house looked finished, but inside, only wooden boards — Ivan said they were called studs — stood where walls should have been. The floor was plain sanded wood like you would see in a good barn. There was no furniture.

"Let me take my two girls on a tour of their new home," said Ivan, grabbing each of us by the hand and grinning with excitement. Marusia tried to paint a smile on her face, but her eyes showed the same confusion that I felt.

"This is our living room," he said. Still holding onto our hands, he walked us through an open doorway. "And this is the bedroom."

Was there only one bedroom in this house? The room was tiny. Barely big enough to fit the two bare mattresses on the floor. Neatly folded bedding was stacked on top. If there was just one bedroom, it would be for Marusia and Ivan.

"Will I be sleeping in the living room, then?" I asked. I wouldn't mind sleeping there. It was more open and airy than this small room.

A look of confusion showed briefly in Ivan's eyes, but then he answered, "When the house is finished, you will have your very own room in the attic." He pointed to a small roughed-out area above our heads. "And you can choose the colour for your walls."

How would I breathe in such a tiny space? Thank goodness it wasn't finished yet. There might be time to change that. "Where will I sleep until then?"

"In the backyard, just like us," Ivan answered.

In the open. Much better!

"Now let us continue the tour."

There wasn't much more to it. Aside from the roughed-out living room and bedroom, there was a kitchen and bathroom and that was it. The bathroom had a sink and a new flush toilet and an old-fashioned iron bathtub with a delicate floral design etched around the edge.

"I got that from the dump," said Ivan proudly. "Can you imagine that someone threw it out?"

A large chunk of enamel was missing from the bottom of the tub, revealing a gash of black metal and a ring of rust. Other than that, the tub was perfectly usable. What I would have given for a tub like this in the camp.

"That is easily fixed," said Ivan, following my glance to the chipped part. "Once the house is finished."

He took us through to the kitchen and we admired the second-hand electric stove with two burners, and a freshly painted baby-blue icebox. Stacked neatly on top of it were three clean but chipped dinner plates and three coffee cups, all different. There was an iron frying pan, and a knife, fork and spoon for each of us. Ivan was most proud of the giant kitchen sink and the taps that ran with hot and cold water. "We can do our laundry in that sink too," he said. "Now wait until you see our backyard."

Ivan let go of my hand long enough to open up the back door. We stepped out onto cinder blocks that had been stacked up to form a step. In the middle of the tiny backyard was a huge oak tree. Hanging from the strongest branch was a rope swing with a wooden seat.

"That is for you, Nadia."

I didn't want to like it, but I couldn't help myself. "Thank you!" I said, and then I hugged Ivan. I really meant it, which surprised me. I ran out to the swing to see it up close. The wooden seat was as smooth as velvet. Ivan had sanded out every stray sliver.

Marusia and Ivan stood hand in hand on the cinder-block porch. "Try it out," she said.

I loved the feel of the breeze on my face as I pumped my legs to make the swing go higher and higher. I felt almost free. When the swing was at its highest, I could see into our neighbours' backyards. Two doors down was another swing in a tree. There was at least one other child on this street, and that was good. Maybe this could be home.

Chapter Two

Is Brantford Home?

That first night, people came to our house with gifts. There was all sorts of food — good rye bread and *holubtsi* and sausage. Marusia was given jars of pickled beets, strawberry jam and honey, as well as eggs and a sack of flour. Someone brought a bolt of light blue cloth and Ivan was given a bottle of vodka. The priest gave me a prayer book, and an English lady with a mole on her cheek gave me a package of crayons. Just as most people were leaving, a couple arrived with an angry looking dark-haired boy in tow. "This is Mychailo," the woman said to me, pushing the boy forward. "He's a student at Central School."

His parents went into the house, leaving Mychailo with me in our yard. "What's Central School?" I asked him.

"You'll be going there in September," he said. "You'll hate it."

"Why?"

"They'll make fun of you because you're not Canadian."

"Do they make fun of you?" I asked.

"Not anymore," he said, balling his hands into fists. "I beat them up if they do."

It didn't seem like something that would work for me. Maybe Mychailo would beat people up for me if we became friends?

After everyone left, Ivan said, "I have another surprise for you." He took my hand and walked me to the bushes that acted as a fence between our yard and our neighbour's. "Did you notice what these are?" he asked.

There were no flowers — the bushes looked like they had just been planted — but I recognized the shape of the leaves. "Lilacs!" I said.

"I planted them for you," he said. "They'll bloom next spring and you'll wake up every morning to their scent."

I was so overcome that I could barely croak out a thank you.

"This is your home, Nadia," he said, giving my hand a squeeze. "We want you to be happy here."

We dragged out the mattresses and slept in the backyard under the stars. The cool breeze soothed me and I loved being in the open. The sound of chirping in the night startled me at first, but Ivan explained that it was the frogs singing, even finding a small one to show me. We had frogs back home but I couldn't remember the last time I saw one. A frog's song is so very different from the sounds of land mines, artillery fire, bombs. How many nights had I tried to sleep despite all those sounds, all through the war years? And the years in the camp, even without the din of war, we had lived so crowded in with other DPs that all I could hear were snores and grunts and sobs.

As I lay there, looking up at the stars and listening to the frogs, I began to relax — just a little. Maybe everything would be fine. I took deep breaths of the cool evening air and closed my eyes, but sleep wouldn't come. Marusia tossed and turned a little bit. She faced me and began to sing the lullaby I had known all my life.

Kolyson'ko, kolyson'ko
Kolyshy nam dytynon'ku
A shchob spalo, ne plakalo
A shchob roslo, ne bolilo
Ni holovka, ni vse tilo

I could feel the fear leave my body as I listened to the words. I was lulled by the cosiness of the mattress and the bedding and being beside the two people who so far had kept me safe.

I fell asleep feeling loved and secure.

I am surrounded by the people whom I love most, snuggled together under a down comforter in a cosy bedroom. Suddenly there is a banging at the door. I try to wake the people beside me but they have melted away. I am alone. My heart pounds. The door bursts open, but I cannot see who it is.

I woke with my arms flailing, shouting, "Leave me alone!" Strong hands pulled me to a sitting position. I opened my eyes. I was in Brantford, in my own backyard. Marusia sat beside me. I was safe. But even in the darkness I could see the worry on her brow. Ivan was there too, kneeling at my other side.

"Were you having a nightmare?" Marusia asked.

It had seemed so real, but yes, it must have been a nightmare. I nodded.

"Do you want to talk about it?"

"No."

Marusia snuggled up close to me on the mattress and whispered the lullaby into my ear in a low sweet voice. The words soothed me a little bit and I could feel my heart settle down.

I wanted to sleep but I didn't want to dream again. Once my breathing slowed, it was easy to convince Marusia that I was all right. She and Ivan needed their sleep.

Marusia settled back on her mattress. I stayed awake, listening to the frogs and the rhythm of Ivan's snores. When I knew that Marusia was also deep in sleep, I sat back up and breathed in some cool night air to try to clear my thoughts. Why did I have that dream? Who was pounding at the door?

I clasped my arms around my knees and rocked back and forth, soothing myself like someone had once soothed me. I chanted the lullaby under my breath. The words made me feel safe and loved. I reached back into my memory, to the last time I had felt completely safe. I remembered a time before the camp. I had a bedroom all to myself then, a room with high ceilings and big windows. I had plenty to eat and good clothing to wear.

But had I felt safe? No. Who could feel safe in the middle of a war?

Chapter Three

Miss MacIntosh

After that nightmare, I tried to stay awake, but exhaustion must have won out, because somehow I slept. When I woke the next morning, I was damp with dew and my neck ached, but I was grateful to be outside and surrounded by clean fresh air. I sat up and stretched and looked over at the other mattress. Marusia was asleep, but Ivan was not there.

Then Marusia opened her eyes and answered my unspoken question. "He's gone to work. And I need to find a job too."

"What will I do?"

"School doesn't start for two months," she replied. "The lady who brought you crayons has offered to help you with your English."

Since there wasn't a kitchen table, we balanced our breakfast plates of fried eggs, jam and rye bread on our knees while sitting on the cinder-block steps. We washed with hot water in the bathroom and Marusia combed the tangles out of my hair and re-wove it into two tight braids. Then she walked me two doors down the street to the house with the swing in the back. She knocked and we waited.

The door opened. "Good morning, Nadia," said the woman in slow and careful English. "My name is Miss MacIntosh."

"Good morning, Miss MacIntosh," I replied, speaking as carefully as I could in English.

The woman turned to Marusia, and in surprisingly good Ukrainian, said, "Hello, Marusia, I hope you had a good first night in your new home."

While the two chatted at the doorstep, I craned my neck to peek inside, but the curtains were drawn and the room was in shadow. A faint scent of lemons and something else wafted out the door.

Marusia mentioned that she would be looking for a job.

"What did you do in Europe?" asked Miss MacIntosh.

Marusia looked flustered. "You mean during the war?"

"Before that," said Miss MacIntosh.

"I was studying to be a pharmacist," said Marusia. "But I will take any kind of job here."

"It will be difficult for you," said Miss MacIntosh in Ukrainian. "Nadia will be fine with me all day."

What? I knew that Marusia would be looking for a job and that I was supposed to learn more English with this woman. But *all day*? I tugged Marusia's hand and looked at her pleadingly.

"Nadia," said Marusia, "Ivan says that Miss MacIntosh has taught English to several children. You will be fine." And then with a determination that shocked me, she pulled her hand from mine and stepped away. "Trust me, Nadia," she said. Then she left.

If I had been younger, I might have run after her, but I

did not want to make a scene. I took a deep breath and swallowed my tears away. I had lived through the war. I could suffer a day with Miss MacIntosh.

Once my eyes had adjusted to the dimness of her living room, I could see that her floor was wooden like ours, but it was mostly covered with a colourfully braided rag rug. The bits of floor that showed at the edges of the room had been varnished and waxed until they gleamed. Her living room was as tiny as ours, but I was amazed at how much furniture she had in it. Beside the door that led to the kitchen was a tall bookcase stuffed with books. Against the other wall was a fireplace with a photo-covered mantle. In the centre was a silver-framed photograph of a sad-looking man in uniform.

"Come and sit here," said Miss MacIntosh, placing her hand gently on my shoulder and leading me to the over-stuffed sofa.

I perched on the edge and Miss MacIntosh drew a book from her shelf and sat down beside me. The book cover was a painting of a girl with blond braids just like mine.

"This is *The Picture Dictionary for Children*," she said, pointing at each word on the cover as she sounded it out.

I love books more than anything. At the camp there were sometimes books in the care packages, but not often ones for children. I longed to touch this book, to hold it up to my face and smell it, but instead I sat still on the sofa beside Miss MacIntosh. She opened the book to a marked page. A drawing of a *yabluko*.

"Apple," said Miss MacIntosh, pointing to each letter as she sounded it out.

"Apple," I said.

She flipped to another marked page. A drawing of a big *aftomobile*. "Automobile," she said, grinning. Almost the same word in English and Ukrainian!

We practised half a dozen words, and then she flipped back to "apple" again and we reviewed them all. We did a few more new ones, and she started back at the beginning again for another review. I knew I wasn't really learning to speak English, I was just learning the English labels for things, but it was fun, doing it with the pictures.

When Miss MacIntosh thought I had learned those first words well enough, we went on to the next six, and the next six after that. I have no idea how long we sat there, but it was likely hours because my bottom was getting numb.

I flipped ahead and was startled by the image of a ferocious looking *pes*. I took a deep breath, then pointed at the letters underneath the picture. "Dog," I said.

"Very good," said Miss MacIntosh, but I think she could tell that the picture had scared me.

"Time for a break," she said as she stood up from the sofa. In Ukrainian, she asked, "Would you like something to eat?"

"Yes please!" I answered in my best English, getting up from the sofa and stretching. I had no idea how long we had been sitting there. Time had seemed to flash by.

As Miss MacIntosh busied herself in the kitchen, I picked up the silver-framed photograph on the mantle. The uniformed man looked young. His uniform was dark and he wore a cap perched at an angle over his right eye . . .

Another mantle . . . another uniform. This one also dark . . .

An image flitted just beyond my grasp as I put the photo

back in its place and turned to the bookcase. Miss MacIntosh's books had colourful spines and the titles were all in English. I longed to pull one out to look at it, but didn't want to do that without permission, so I stepped just inside the kitchen and watched her.

"You can sit there," she said, pointing to one of her kitchen chairs.

She set two glasses of milk on the table, two empty soup bowls and two empty plates. She opened the cupboard and took out a red and white can and opened it. She slid the jiggly contents into a saucepan and added a can of water.

Miss MacIntosh didn't have an icebox like us, but a refrigerator. As she opened it and took out an orange block of something, a bit of the cooled air escaped and enveloped my face.

Miss MacIntosh sliced some pieces off the orange block and arranged the squares on slices of — Wonder Bread! I thought I had seen the last of Wonder Bread, but it was not to be.

"Please, what is that?" I asked in English, pointing to the block of orange.

"Velveeta," answered Miss MacIntosh.

"Velveeta," I repeated, letting the unusual word roll out on my tongue.

"It is a kind of cheese," said Miss MacIntosh, in Ukrainian.

"Oh!"

She set slices of Wonder Bread onto a cookie sheet, with the pieces of Velveeta on top, then slid the sheet into the oven. Steam rose from the soup. "It is ready," she said.

She pulled out the cookie sheet and brought it over to the table, then slid an open-faced cheese sandwich onto each of our plates. I watched my bowl fill with red as she ladled out soup for each of us.

This soup was like nothing I had ever seen. Soup was a staple in the camp. Usually it was mostly water with some cabbage and potato, but every once in a while there would be a bit of meat. This soup was thick like gravy. I took a small spoonful and placed it on my tongue. A tangy sweet tomato taste. Not bad, but not really soup, either.

I smiled at Miss MacIntosh. "Good!" I said.

She nodded in approval.

The sandwich was another matter. I had never seen cheese quite that colour before and the fact that it was on Wonder Bread didn't help. I picked up the sandwich with my fingertips and took a small bite. The bread was toasty from the oven and the cheese had a pleasant, gooey texture. Miss MacIntosh was watching me expectantly. I swallowed down the bite, grateful — as always — for any food . . .

Marusia and I are sprawled on an open flatcar in the blackest part of the night. Other escapees too, all holding on as the train chugs along at an alarming speed. It slows to a stop. I sit up and watch in horror as Marusia jumps off and runs into a farmer's field. She is scrabbling in the dry earth, digging with her bare hands. I hear her hoot for joy. She runs back and jumps onto the flatcar. "Potatoes," she says. "Two of them!"

One of the other fugitives brings a pot out of a tattered bag and someone makes a small fire from gathered twigs in

the middle of the flatcar. Another man who has run into the
field comes back with his hat filled with muddy water. He
dumps it into the pot. Marusia adds her potatoes.

The steam of the cooking potatoes makes my stomach
grumble. I have had nothing to eat for days.

This is the first time the train has stopped since we've
taken refuge on the flatcar. The potatoes are barely cooked
through but we cannot wait. We have no idea how long the
train will remain still and we're afraid the smell of fire will
bring soldiers.

One man has a spoon tucked away in his frayed coat. He
takes it out reverently and dips it into our soup and gives me
— the only child — the first spoonful. It is the best soup I
have ever tasted. The spoon is passed around like a sacra-
ment. Within minutes, every drop is consumed. The train
starts moving just as we're finishing . . .

I felt a hand on my shoulder and was startled back into
the present. Miss MacIntosh looked at me with concern.

Tears welled up in my eyes. I rubbed them from my
face with the back of my hand and avoided Miss
MacIntosh's stare. These random images made me confused, and angry with myself.

Miss MacIntosh finished her own soup and sandwich
and then I stacked the dirty dishes and cutlery and began
to carry them to the sink.

"You don't have to do that," said Miss MacIntosh, taking the dishes from my hands.

"But I would like to help you," I said, knowing that
Marusia would expect nothing less. And the busy work
helped me shake away the memory. I stood beside Miss
MacIntosh as she filled the sink with hot sudsy water.

"Okay," she said, handing me a dishtowel. "You can dry."

I took each plate as she placed in on the rack and dried it carefully, admiring the delicate pattern of matching pink roses as I placed them in her cupboard. The pieces were smooth and light to the touch. Not at all like the mismatched cups and plates that Ivan had found for us.

Miss MacIntosh drained the water from the sink and wiped the counter dry. "There," she said. "All done. I think it's time for a treat." She set out some small brown cookies on a plate. "Gingersnaps," she said, motioning me to sit back down at the table.

"Gingersnaps," I repeated. It was a nice word, but didn't exactly roll off the tongue.

They looked like *medvinyky* — honey cookies. I picked one up and sniffed it. They did not smell like honey. They smelled of that other scent that I had noticed when I first arrived at Miss MacIntosh's house. I took tiny a bite. The cookie was crispy like a honey cookie, but its taste was like biting into a memory . . .

The blond woman has her servant make cookies with a sweet yet peppery taste. And they are shaped like men. Gingerbread men. I bite off the head and swallow it down, and then an arm and a leg. I stare at the half-eaten cookie and feel ill. "Eat," the blond woman says.

The gingersnap was a dry lump in the back of my throat. I looked up. Miss MacIntosh was watching me intently again. I tried to swallow but nearly choked. I gulped down some milk and the cookie slid down my throat.

"Good," I said weakly. Miss MacIntosh smiled.

There was a tap-tapping at the kitchen door. Had

Marusia given up on her job search and come to get me?

Miss MacIntosh opened the door. It wasn't Marusia. It was that boy from last night — Mychailo.

He looked from Miss MacIntosh to me. He frowned.

"You can come in," said Miss MacIntosh. "I have cookies."

Mychailo stepped in, then plopped himself down in one of the spare kitchen chairs. "Is she teaching you English already?" he asked me in Ukrainian.

"Ask her in English, Mychailo," said Miss MacIntosh.

Mychailo rolled his eyes and reached for a cookie. He popped it whole into his mouth and hardly chewed at all before swallowing. He looked at me and said in painfully slow and loud English, "Are you learning to speak English, Nadia?"

"*Tak.*"

Miss MacIntosh gave me a look.

"Yes," I said. "I am learning to speak English."

Miss MacIntosh nodded with approval. "When you've finished your snack, you two can play in the backyard for a bit if you like."

I didn't know whether I wanted to play with Mychailo. What I longed to do was to go back into Miss MacIntosh's living room and look at her books.

Mychailo gulped down his milk and looked at me. "Let's go," he said in English, pointing to the back door.

Miss MacIntosh's swing was just like mine, but the wood was darker and more worn. Did she swing on this herself? How funny it would be to see a grown woman on a swing!

She was standing at the back door, watching us, so

Mychailo said in careful English, "Nadia, sit, and I will push you."

Miss MacIntosh nodded in approval, then went back inside.

I sat down on the swing and pumped with my legs a little to get the rhythm going, and then Mychailo pushed so hard that it took my breath away. "Be gentle," I said in Ukrainian.

"You'll never learn if you keep speaking Ukrainian!" said Mychailo, in a voice that mimicked Miss MacIntosh.

"You are hurting me."

Either he didn't understand my English or he didn't care. Each time the swing brought me close to him, he pushed hard on my back. The swing went so high that I was afraid it would loop around and get tangled in the branches of the tree. Yet with each push, I felt the wind in my face and the freedom of flying in the air. "STOP!"

"If that's what you want," said Mychailo, stepping away from the swing. He plopped down on the lawn and combed the grass with his fingers, ignoring me completely.

I stretched out my feet and dragged them along the ground to slow the swing down, but it was going so fast that I lost one shoe. I panicked and jumped, landing flat on my face in the lawn.

"You are so stupid," said Mychailo. He continued to comb through the blades of grass while I dusted myself off.

The back door opened and Miss MacIntosh stood there. "Lesson time in ten minutes," she said.

I flopped down on the grass beside Mychailo. "Are

you getting English lessons too?" I asked.

"Yes," he said. "I come here every afternoon."

"But your English is already good," I said.

"My parents like me to come, and Miss MacIntosh is a nice lady, so I don't mind. And she makes good cookies."

I mulled this over. Did it mean that I would be coming here every day as well? If I learned quickly, would I only have to come in the afternoons? I also didn't know how I felt about spending so much time with Mychailo.

"Where did you live before the war?" asked Mychailo.

His question took me by surprise. "In . . . in . . . Zolochiv."

Mychailo rolled his eyes. "You are such a bad liar."

He was right. I was lying. But what he didn't realize was that I had lived a lie for so long that I couldn't remember where I had really come from. The lying had come naturally at the camp. If I hadn't done it then, they would have taken me away from Marusia. But something strange had begun to happen since coming to Canada. I was beginning to have flashes from the past, like the ones today, but they were like pieces of a jigsaw puzzle that didn't fit.

"What makes you think I'm lying?" I asked.

"You have a funny accent," he said. "My parents were born in Zolochiv. Ivan is from Zolochiv. But you are definitely from somewhere else."

It scared me to think that this boy knew more about my past than I did. "Was Ivan . . . I mean . . . my father . . . a friend of your parents?" I asked.

"My father was in the underground with Ivan," said Mychailo. "They fought the Nazis together."

He said nothing more for a while, but instead concentrated on raking the grass with his hands. "That's what you remind me of," he said.

"What?" I asked.

"With that hair of yours and those eyes? A Nazi."

And then without a glance at me, he stood up and walked into the house.

Chapter Four

Am I a Nazi?

I felt strange spending the rest of the afternoon with Mychailo after his Nazi remark. It got me wondering though. At the DP camp, most people could speak many languages, but no one sounded quite like me. When we first arrived, some people had commented that I didn't sound like my mother and we didn't look like each other, but Marusia would always hush them.

Miss MacIntosh had Mychailo do Composition at the kitchen table and she continued to go through the word book with me. I was glad that he wasn't working right beside me.

Whenever we paused, I would glance up at the photograph of the soldier on Miss MacIntosh's mantle. Once, she followed my gaze and sighed. "I was going to marry him," she said. "He died in France, fighting the Nazis."

What did Miss MacIntosh think of me? With my blond hair and blue eyes and funny way of talking, did she think I was a Nazi too? That I was responsible for her fiancé's death? My throat choked with tears.

Marusia thought it would be good for me to remember

all that I could about the time before we met. She always insisted that I had nothing to feel guilty about. I tried to remember, but all that came to me were bits and pieces. Nothing that made sense. It was all so confusing. I looked up at this kind lady, Miss MacIntosh, and said, "I am sorry he died."

Even though the war hadn't come to Canada, her fiancé had gone to the war. I guess this is why it was called a world war.

The afternoon sped by. I was so caught up in learning the new words that when there was a tapping on the front door, I jumped in surprise. When Miss MacIntosh opened the door, there stood Marusia, looking sad and tired.

Miss MacIntosh let me take the word book home so that Marusia and Ivan and I could all practise our English together. I slipped my hand into Marusia's and gave it a squeeze as we walked down the street. She looked at me, startled. Her eyes filled with tears, but she smiled. "I will find a job," she said. "Don't you worry."

That made me smile. For as long as I could remember, all I did was live day by day. It meant that I didn't worry. But it also meant that I had stopped hoping.

As we walked down the street hand in hand, Marusia looked at me. "What is the matter, Nadia?" she asked.

I didn't say anything for a bit. We had been through this all before, but then I blurted out, "I'm a Nazi, aren't I?"

Marusia stopped walking. She turned and looked me in the eye. "No, *Sonechko*, you are *not* a Nazi."

"Am I German?"

Marusia shook her head.

"Then why do I look like a Nazi?" I asked. "The other

children in the DP camp didn't look like me and they didn't sound like me. Mychailo sounds different than me. *You* sound different from me."

Marusia's eyes filled with tears. "Has Mychailo said something to you?"

I don't like to snitch and I don't like to lie. "He and I don't sound the same."

"You are not a Nazi and you are not German," she said firmly.

"But I remember the place that you stole me from!" I said.

Marusia put one hand on her hip and pointed a finger at me. "Have I ever treated you unkindly?"

"No."

"Have I treated you like anything less than I would if you were my own flesh?"

"No."

"Then trust me when I tell you that I never stole you and you are not a Nazi."

She reached out to grab my hand but I held it behind my back. I was furious with her, although I didn't quite know why. We walked the rest of the way home in silence.

When we got to our house, we saw a truck filled with sheets of plywood parked in front of it. Two men that I recognized from the night before — one of them Mychailo's father — were unloading wood from the back of the truck. A third man was holding our front door open.

"Come on, let's see what they're doing!" I said to Marusia.

We followed the men into the living room. I blinked in surprise. Just yesterday, this space was nothing more than bare wooden frames, but now plywood sheets had been nailed over the framework, making it an enclosed room. I stepped into the bedroom. Ivan had taken his shirt off and his back glistened with sweat. He was kneeling in the corner, carefully hammering in small nails along one side of a piece of plywood that another man held in place. Three walls of the bedroom were already covered.

Before the walls went up, the house had seemed open and airy and free. I wish it could have stayed like that. But I breathed in deeply the scent of fresh sawdust and pasted a smile onto my face for Ivan.

He looked up when he heard us step in. "Here are my girls," he said, grinning.

"You are such a fast builder!" said Marusia.

"I wanted to have the walls up before you got to Brantford," said Ivan. "But I've been working overtime the past few weeks and the days got away from me." He gestured towards the other men. "What would I do without my good friends?"

"You all must be hungry," said Marusia. "We shall make you something to eat."

The sound of nails echoed through the kitchen as I helped Marusia put something quick together. Once the men had eaten and finished up their work, they left, promising to be back the next day.

Ivan and Marusia sat on the cinder-block step, sipping mugs of tea after everyone had left. I sat on my swing and listened to their conversation.

"When do you sleep, Ivashko?" Marusia asked, brushing his forehead with her fingertips. "You barely closed your eyes last night before it was time for you to get up."

"I will sleep once the house is finished," said Ivan.

"Can you take a rest now?" asked Marusia. "Why don't you lie down on the mattress?"

"It's still light out," he protested. "I can get some more work done on the house."

"Come." Marusia took his hand. "We'll lie down for a few minutes together. Just to rest our eyes."

I wanted to give them some time on their own. After all, they hadn't been married for very long, and they had been apart for a year. I got up from the swing and headed towards the front yard.

"Where are you going?" called Marusia.

"Exploring," I called back, trying hard to look happy.

"Stay in the neighbourhood," she said. "And come home before it gets dark."

I smiled to myself at that. Did Marusia really think I would go very far? I sat on the front steps for a while and looked up and down the street. Maybe I would just sit here for an hour. I could hear children playing in the distance and a car or two passed. Once, a man wearing a suit and carrying a lunch box walked by. He tipped his hat to me and smiled, so I smiled back. That small gesture made me feel safer, I don't know why. Maybe this new life we had invented would be all right.

Mychailo had said that Central School was down the street from me. It couldn't be very far. I took a deep breath and stood up. I am a Canadian girl now, I told myself. And Canadian girls walk down the street by themselves without fear.

I forced myself to walk away from the house and down the street. I felt a little bit scared to be doing this, but I was proud of myself too. And the soft breeze on my face felt good. I walked past Miss MacIntosh's house until I got to George Street and then I saw what had to be the school: a huge old yellow brick building two and a half storeys high, with a circular driveway in the front and a huge lawn.

There weren't many buildings this big left standing in Germany. It felt eerily safe to be walking in this unfamiliar area all by myself. There were no bombs, no men in uniform, no burnt-out buildings, no barbed wire.

I walked up to one of the windows and peered in. It was a classroom with rows of desks and various posters pinned to the wall. This one had a portrait of King George above the chalkboard — I recognized it from some of the coins I'd seen.

Which rulers had been on the walls of my other classrooms? I drew a blank. I sat down in the grass and leaned against the wall of the school. It wasn't time to go home yet. Perhaps I could walk just a bit farther? Three blocks away was a beautiful park, a church, and some rich looking buildings across the road.

The building beside the church caught my eye. It had four marble pillars and a set of white steps leading up to fancy double doors on the second floor. I walked up the steps and stood on my toes so I could peer through the glass. I could see a marble entranceway, and beyond that, a room lined with books. How I longed to touch those books. To smell them . . .

"It's the library," said a familiar voice behind me.

"Why did you creep up on me like that?" I said, turning to face Mychailo.

He had a silly look on his face. "I didn't," he said. "You just didn't hear me."

I tried to stare him down, but then noticed that he was holding a thick book.

"Did you get that from in there?" I asked.

"It is a library," he said. "What do you think?"

"How much did it cost?"

"It's free for me to read," he said. "As long as I return it."

"Who gets to use the library?" I asked.

"Anyone," he said. "You just have to fill out a form and they give you a library card. Then you can take out books as often as you want, as long as you return them after you've read them."

"Who decides what books you can read?"

"It's not like that in Canada," said Mychailo. "You can read any book in the children's department, as long as you have a library card."

"Can I go in now?"

"It just closed," he said. "But do you want to go tomorrow after our class with Miss MacIntosh?"

I was beginning to warm to Mychailo. He could be rough and rude, but that could be said of any boy. This one liked books.

Chapter Five

Eva

I would have liked to sleep outside under the stars again, but angry clouds had formed in the sky just as the sun was setting. We swept up the sawdust, and Ivan dragged one mattress out to the middle of the living room.

"It's almost like you're outside," said Marusia. "This is a big room. And if you need us, we're right in there." She pointed to the bedroom. The look in her eyes told me that she was exhausted, and I knew that Ivan was even more tired, so I smiled and said that I would be fine. I took Miss MacIntosh's word book to bed with me and looked at the pictures and tried to sound out the words until it got dark.

The rain pounding on the rooftop muffled out the sound of the frogs — or maybe frogs sleep inside during the rain too? The rain was comforting, but the distant grumbling of thunder reminded me of gunfire.

The windows were bare, so when a car passed, strange shapes played across the walls. I closed my eyes and concentrated on breathing deeply and hoped I would fall asleep quickly.

I am snuggled under a down comforter, surrounded by

people who love me. I hear pounding on my door. I try to snuggle in and hide behind the others, but they've melted away. I am alone. More pounding at the door. A child's voice asking me to open up. Who is that child, and why does her voice terrify me?

I sat up with a jolt. Where was I? A frog chirped. I looked around in the darkness and saw moonlight coming in through the window. Rain still pounded on the rooftop. I was in Ivan's house in Brantford. This room had no furniture and smelled of freshly sanded wood. I was safe here. I wrapped my arms around my legs and rocked myself back and forth. I felt like screaming but I didn't know why. I closed my eyes and chanted the *kolysanka* under my breath.

Who was the girl I had dreamt of? I did not want to go back to sleep and I did not want to wake up Ivan and Marusia, so I tiptoed into the kitchen and poured myself a glass of water. I sat down at the table and watched the raindrops on the kitchen window. I wanted to remember that time. If I could figure out the puzzle, maybe the nightmares would go away. Marusia said I had nothing to be ashamed of. But how could she know that for sure? I stared out the window again, still thinking of that girl . . .

I am in the bedroom with the high ceiling. Raindrops trickle outside pink-curtained windows and I see the beginning of daylight peeking around the edges. There is a tap-tapping on the door.

It flies open and Eva bounds in. "Sister, you should be up by now!" She scrambles up onto my bed. "Wear your new pink dress," she says. "Then we'll match."

I watch her chubby feet as she slides off the bed and skips out the door. No one looking at us together would ever think that we match, even if we are both dressed in pink. I stay in bed for a moment longer. Why do I not feel safe in this room? It is all a girl could hope for, with its pink ruffled curtains and soft four-poster bed. A wooden box in the corner brims with stuffed toys. On the wall across from the bed is a high shelf holding a row of perfectly blond, blue-eyed dolls — all gifts from Vater. I do not like them.

As I get out of bed, one foot lands on the sharp corner of a book. I bend down and pick it up: Der Giftpiltz — The Poisonous Mushroom. *Another gift from Vater that I do not like. It slips out of my hands and crashes back to the floor. I brush the wrinkles out of my nightgown and walk barefoot to the bathroom. The air is damp and the mirror is covered with steam. Mutter must have just got up herself. She is probably waiting in the dining room for Eva and me.*

I grab my toothbrush, smear it with dental paste and give my teeth a quick brushing. I splash water on my face, making sure to dampen my soap bar so it looks like I used it, and then dry off with the pink towel that is stitched with GH, *just like my other towels.*

A crack of thunder jolted me out of the past. For just a second, the kitchen was daylight-bright from lightning. The scene in my mind was still so vivid that I could almost feel the grit of dental paste on my tongue. I took a slow sip from the glass of water on the table in front of me and tried to remember more, but the moment had passed. Was that girl — Eva — my sister? Why did I not love her?

There was nothing in that memory that was frightening, so why did it scare me so? And what did *GH* stand for? I did not want to go back to sleep, so I stayed sitting at the table and watched the rain and more lightning through the kitchen window. I had enough food and fine clothing back then. I had Mutter and Vater and Eva. Why was I not happy?

It was still dark when I heard the creak of footsteps on the wooden floor and the sound of the bathroom door swinging open — Ivan was getting ready for work. Through the kitchen window there was now a bare glimmer of morning light. I could see the outline of the swing, shimmering with rain. I remembered how happy Ivan was when he surprised me with it. Maybe I could surprise him now. I walked over to the sink and filled the kettle with water for tea and put it on a burner. I found the frying pan, set it on the other burner, took out some bacon from the icebox and placed it in the frying pan. As the bacon sizzled, I cracked two eggs into the pan.

By the time the bathroom door opened, breakfast was waiting on the table at Ivan's spot.

He came into the kitchen in his work shirt and pants, smelling of soap and with his wet hair combed back. "Nadia," he said, glancing first at me and then at the plate of food. "What a surprise."

I could tell from the look in his eyes that he had a thousand questions. "I couldn't sleep," I told him. "And I wanted to do something special for you."

Ivan walked up behind my chair. He hugged my shoulders and kissed the top of my head. "You are such a sweet girl," he said. "Thank you."

"Eat," I told him, swallowing back tears. "It will get cold."

Ivan ate quickly and gulped down his tea. I knew that

he didn't want to be late for work. After he left, I washed the dishes and prepared breakfast for Marusia and myself.

✤ ✤ ✤

I took the word book with me when Marusia dropped me off at Miss MacIntosh's house after breakfast and we practised new words and phrases. Mychailo came after lunch, just as he'd done the day before, but he seemed somehow nicer. He sat at the kitchen table with a workbook while I sat in the living room with Miss MacIntosh. Hours flew by.

"You learn so quickly, Nadia," she said with a smile. She took the word book from my lap and closed it, then set it on the coffee table. "Would you like to take this book home again with you?"

"Yes please," I said.

"Why don't I take her to the library today?" Mychailo said from the kitchen. "Then she'd get to practise her English with different books."

Miss MacIntosh's face brightened. "What a lovely idea, Mychailo. If Marusia comes back before you two are finished at the library, I'll tell her where you are."

Mychailo didn't take me directly to the library. Instead, we walked around downtown for a bit. He showed me the movie theatre, the market square and the city hall. There was a long grey car parked out in front of city hall. "I think that's the mayor's," said Mychailo.

When we got to the library, we went up the big white steps to the glass doors and opened them. I was enveloped by a *whoosh* of cool air and the scent of books and furniture polish.

"The children's department is this way," said Mychailo, taking me to a set of inside stairs that went down to the basement. We walked up to a long counter in the middle of the main room. For a library, this room had surprisingly few books. The walls were wood-panelled and empty of shelves.

"Can't we go in there?" I said, pointing to the room on the left that was filled with books.

"We've got to find Miss Barry first," said Mychailo. "You need to get a library card."

Just then, a pretty woman with blond curls and blue-framed glasses came in. "Good to see you, Mychailo," she said. "So you've brought a friend."

"This is Nadia."

I did a little curtsey and said, "Hello, Miss Barry."

"Nadia needs a library card," said Mychailo. "I can help her with the form."

Miss Barry went behind the counter and looked through the drawers. She handed me a pencil and a sheet of paper with questions and lines on it. "I need a phone number and address."

My heart sank. "We do not have a phone," I said. Did that mean that I couldn't have a library card?

Mychailo took the form from my hand. "I'll fill it out," he said. "And I'll put in the phone number of the foundry where your father works — my father works there too so I know the number."

"Thank you, Mychailo!"

He led me into the room on the left. "These are good ones to start with," he said.

I gasped as I stepped into the room. All four walls were covered with shelves of books, and there were aisles of books as well . . .

A long-ago room filled with books, so many books, but I was forbidden to touch them . . .

"This is a good one for you to start with," Mychailo said. He handed me a book and read the title out loud, *The Little Engine That Could.* "I'll be in the other room for a while, so come and find me if you get bored."

I held the book up to my face and breathed in its lovely scent of ink and glue. It seemed hard to believe that I would be allowed to take a book home from this place. I opened it up. The images in this story niggled at my memory. A train chugging along . . . boxes of toys . . . a blond doll with blue eyes . . . Maybe this wasn't the book for me. I put it back on the shelf and pulled out one that had a painting of three little kittens on the front. Using the pictures as clues, I read as much as I could while I stood there . . . *kittens, mittens, cry.*

I did the same with a few more books. How would I ever choose? I put them all back on the shelf and wandered into the other room. These books were thicker and they didn't have as many pictures. I found Mychailo sitting in a corner, surrounded by books.

"Which one are you going to take out?" I asked him.

He looked up at me and then back down at the books on the floor. "I think I'll take *Tom Sawyer* today," he said. "Aren't you getting one?"

"I can't decide," I said.

"I'll show you some that I liked when I first came to Brantford," he said. He stacked the books from the floor and set them on a wheeled cart. With *Tom Sawyer* tucked in the crook of his arm, he walked to the picture-book room with me following close behind.

"Here's a good one," he said, reaching up and grabbing an oversized book from a shelf at the back. "It will help teach you the words for numbers in English."

It was a counting book very similar to Miss MacIntosh's word book. "Thanks, Mychailo," I said. "This is perfect."

❖ ❖ ❖

When I got back home, Ivan was stretched out on the floor in our living room, carefully tapping nails into a narrow strip of wood along the bottom of the wall. "Can I get you anything?" I asked him.

Ivan looked up from his work and smiled. "I would love some water."

I went into the kitchen and set my library book on the table. I filled a glass with tap water and brought it out to the living room for Ivan. He drank it down quickly and handed the glass back to me.

When I took it back to the kitchen, I stood for a moment and stared out of the window. I could see my own reflection there. My face, my eyes, my braids . . .

I am wearing the pink dress. The sight of it makes me feel sick.

When I get downstairs, Mutter is at the dining room table. Cook has served her porridge and Eva is halfway through hers. On the table is a crystal serving dish filled with berries, apples and grapes.

Cook places a bowl in front of me, sprinkled with cinnamon and sugar. Even so, I hate it.

"The rally is in less than an hour," says Mutter, her eyes sparkling with excitement. "Eat quickly."

Eva shovels the last of her porridge into her mouth and swallows it down. She puts her spoon on the table with a clatter and stands up. "I'm finished!"

"Go get your hairbrush," says Mutter. "I'll fix your hair as soon as your sister and I finish our breakfast."

I swallow the cereal as quickly as I can, not caring so much what it tastes like but just to get it over with. Eva comes back with pink hair ribbons and a hairbrush and a hand mirror.

Mutter brushes out the tangles from Eva's dark blond hair until it hangs down her back in shiny waves. She expertly makes two braids, finishing each off with a pink ribbon.

When it is my turn she tugs at my hair and braids it up more tightly than she needs to. "There," she says with a cold edge in her voice. She hands me the mirror. "Don't you look lovely?"

The face that looks back at me is the same one as always. I never think of myself as lovely.

A long black car with two small swastika flags along the side of the hood idles in the driveway as we walk outside. A uniformed man opens the back door. Mutter gets in first, then Eva, then me. The upholstery is lush black leather that gleams from a fresh buffing. The car door is closed with a firm click and we speed away.

It takes half an hour of fast driving to get into the city. The streets narrow. Our driver slows down so we can wave to the blocks and blocks of cheering crowds.

When we get within walking distance of the stage, the car stops. Soldiers push the crowd away so we can get out, and then they lead us to the steps on the side of the stage. Most of the chairs are taken by Nazi officers, but there are a few other mothers and children as well. We take our spots in the front row, behind the podium.

The crowd roars as another long black car pulls up. When the führer *steps out, the crowd goes wild.* Vater *gets out of the car just behind the* führer.

The crowd chants "Heil Hitler! Heil Hitler!" *as the* führer *steps onto the stage, but it is as if he doesn't notice. He walks up to me and crouches down until we are eye level. He is so close to me that I can see his nose hair and smell the slightly spicy scent of his hair pomade.* "What a perfect specimen of Aryan youth you are, my dear," *he says, pinching my cheek. I smile. What else can I do?* Vater *stands behind the* führer, *bursting with pride, but Eva looks like she is about to cry and* Mutter's *lips are a thin white line.* Vater *sits down between Eva and Mutter. He grabs* Mutter's *hand and kisses it.*

The führer *walks to the podium and begins to . . .*

"Nadia, what are you doing?"

I nearly jumped out of my skin at the sound of Marusia's voice. The empty glass almost shot out of my hand. I blinked twice. I was standing in front of the window in the kitchen of the Brantford house.

I turned to Marusia. She stood by the table, with Ivan beside her, his hammer in one hand and a look of concern on his face.

I shook my head, desperate to clear away the image of Hitler's face. If I'd met Hitler — *Hitler* himself — then I must be a Nazi. What secret was Marusia keeping from me? Who *was* I?

My face was wet with tears, but I couldn't remember crying. My legs felt wobbly, so I set the glass beside the sink and sat down at the table.

Marusia walked behind my chair. She wrapped her arms protectively around me and rested her head on my neck.

Ivan knelt beside us.

"Are you all right?" he asked. His eyes were round with fright.

"I was just thinking," I told them.

"You were shouting, '*Heil Hitler*,'" said Ivan, a troubled look in his eyes.

"What were you thinking about?" asked Marusia.

"The farmhouse and that family," I said. "But there was more."

"Do you want to talk about it?" she asked.

"No!" Couldn't she understand how ashamed I was? Marusia insisted that I wasn't a Nazi, but that's not what my memory was telling me. How I wished I could wash away that horrible past.

"You need to air these memories, Nadia," said Ivan. "And until you remember it all, you'll keep on having nightmares."

Was Ivan right? Maybe he was . . .

"Would it help if I told you about what happened to *me* during the war?" he asked. He straddled the chair facing me and looked into my eyes.

Ivan's offer surprised me. He never talked about his past. "I would like to hear what you did during the war," I told him.

For a minute he said nothing and I saw his eyes fill with tears as his memories came drifting into his mind. He blinked the tears back and took a breath. "My story is one like so many others. The Soviets killed my father and brother in 1941. They were killing thousands of the men, even some of the women and children. I wasn't arrested with them — I thought at the time that I was lucky — but then the Nazis came."

Ivan's eyes met mine and I could feel my face flush with shame. He looked up at Marusia, who still stood behind me, her arms wrapped around me. Ivan gave a ragged sigh. "I thought nothing could compare to the Soviets, but I was wrong. The Nazis were just as bad. My sister was captured in a Nazi slave raid. My mother was sent to a concentration camp. I was the last of my family. I joined the underground. Sometimes we fought the Nazis and sometimes we fought the Soviets. It depended on which front was closest. I escaped to a DP camp just as the war was ending."

So much sadness in so few words. "I am sorry, Ivan." I could feel tears spilling down my cheeks.

"I needed to say that out loud," said Ivan. "And you should talk to us about what *you* remember." He gave me a long bear hug.

Maybe he was right. I just couldn't do it yet.

We were silent for a long time, each of us wrapped in our own thoughts. As I sat there, I tried to piece together what I now remembered about my past. The rich farmhouse and a bedroom filled with toys. A pink dress that I hated — why would I hate it so? Towels stitched with *GH*. What did *GH* stand for? Were Mutter, Vater and Eva my real family? The scene of meeting Hitler face to face was etched in my brain — how I wished I could scrub that away, but it was vivid, right down to his smell.

Ivan hated the Nazis. Look what they did to his mother

and sister. If I was a Nazi, then how could Ivan love me? How could anyone love me?

But how could I argue with these flashes from the past? My name wasn't really Nadia, but something starting with G. The farmhouse, the long black car and Hitler — these images were like photographs in my mind.

I knew how easily Marusia could lie. Was she lying to me about my past?

Chapter Six

Lilacs

Summer went by quickly. Marusia got a job picking straw-berries. When strawberry season was over, the same farmer hired her to work on his other crops. My days were taken up with lessons at Miss MacIntosh's house and vis-its to the library with Mychailo. Miss Barry grinned when-ever she saw us. She would let us look at the new arrivals and would point out books that she thought we might like. The routine of the summer seemed to settle my mind. The flashbacks and nightmares seemed to go away.

❖ ❖ ❖

On Saturday nights, if Ivan wasn't too tired, he, Marusia and I would walk to the hall on Dundas Street. It was a rented building shared by all the Ukrainians in town — Catholic and Orthodox alike. Marusia especially loved it when we went out like this. For working on the farm she wore a used pair of men's overalls and she would change into a second-hand housedress when she got home. But for Saturday nights, she wore her one nice blouse and skirt.

Sometimes people at the hall would get together a

band and there would be a dance. Other times, people would sit at tables and talk. Marusia would sit with a group who were writing letters to relief organizations, trying to find lost loved ones. They would update each other on their progress and compare notes.

I liked to go because there were other children who spoke Ukrainian. Mychailo would often be there. I was devastated to learn that none of the other Ukrainian children except for Mychailo would be attending Central School. There weren't that many of us and we were spread all over the city. There were two sisters who had been born in Canada. Their Ukrainian was not good. They went to Grandview. And a tall boy with glasses who spoke Ukrainian with a Polish accent was going to start at St. Basil's School.

Early each Sunday morning we would dress again in our good clothing and walk to the Ukrainian Catholic church on Terrace Hill Street, which was one block closer than the hall. It was a small church and there were so many people who attended that we had to get there early if we wanted to get a pew. The only inside place where I felt completely safe was sitting in that church. Few parishioners could sing on key, but that didn't bother me. I loved being enveloped in the hymns and I loved the smell of the incense. It made me feel protected.

Ivan worked on the house every day after work, and by the last week in August, it was finished. Each morning Marusia got picked up by a truck to take her to the farm in Burford. The money was needed, but her hands were swollen from the long hours of working in the fields.

I knew it was more than just her hands and the long

hours that bothered her, though. Whenever the postman delivered mail, she looked through the envelopes with a hungry eye, but he never seemed to bring whatever she was waiting for. I asked her about it once, but her eyes filled with tears. "I cannot talk about it now," was all she told me. I think she was hoping to get news from the Red Cross about a relative. At the hall, when someone got one of these letters, everyone gathered round to hear it read aloud. Sometimes the news was bad, but when it was good, we all hooted for joy.

Marusia had once studied to be a pharmacist, but as a slave labourer during the war, she worked in a factory. Later on she was forced to work as a cook at the German farm where we met. How awful it was for her to have to do hard labour again, even though she was supposed to be free. I would see a troubled look come over her face from time to time. Whenever I asked her what was wrong, she'd paste on a smile and say, "Nothing, Nadia. I was just thinking."

As often as we could, the three of us would sit down together on the cinder blocks in the backyard and pore over the books from the library and from Miss MacIntosh. Marusia's dream was to learn English well enough to get a job in a store or maybe even a pharmacy. Ivan's spoken English was good, but he had no way of learning how to write it. I think he was looking forward to me starting school because then I could teach him everything I learned.

The week before school was to start, Ivan greeted me at the door when I came in from Miss MacIntosh's. He had a grin on his face. "The day has come to choose the colour of your room."

No, no, no. I had become used to sleeping in the living

room on cold or rainy nights, and outside when the weather was hot.

"I don't need a bedroom," I said. "Why don't I sleep in the living room always?" He looked at me with one eyebrow raised. "Then you could use that upstairs room for storage."

He shook his head. "Nadia, you need your own room."

I said nothing. Ivan caught my hand in his and led me out the door. "You'll see," he said. "In time you'll like having a bedroom again."

The paint store was on Colborne Street — two big blocks around the corner from the library. Ivan held the door open with one hand and made a sweeping motion with his other. I stepped in. The wet paint smell tugged at the edges of my memory but, thankfully, no images came.

Shiny metal cans were stacked against the walls and in the aisles. I expected to see different colours, but the cans were mostly covered with white labels. On a stand beside the cashier's counter was a book of colour chips. Ivan led me to it. He flipped it open at random and the page revealed shades of yellow and gold. He looked at me expectantly, but I shook my head. Yellow meant sunshine and I loved sunshine, but yellow made me sad . . .

I am in that long black car. It is just me and Vater and the chauffeur. We are taken to a cluster of buildings surrounded by barbed wire. The sign at the entrance says Work Shall Set You Free. *The gates open and the chauffeur drives in. I feel sick. Vater grabs my hand and pulls me out of the car as he gets out.*

He leads me past a snaking line of hungry-eyed women and children. Some wear heavy clothing and others are dressed for summer. They all wear one thing in common: a yellow hand-stitched star. A girl my age is in a yellow dress that once was beautiful. Maybe her mother thought a yellow star wouldn't show on a yellow dress. As we pass, the girl looks me in the eye.

"Don't stare at them," says Vater, pulling me by the hand. We step into a storage area beyond the lineup. Crates and boxes brim over with fancy clothing: fur coats, blue satin slippers, a tiara — even what looks like a new wedding gown. A well-fed man sitting behind a desk doesn't get up when we enter, but he nods as if he is expecting us. My heart pounds with fear. Is Vater angry with me? Is he leaving me here? I have no yellow star.

The man grins at me as he looks me up and down. His teeth are yellow and his uniform collar is so tight that his neck bulges. "You must be Gretchen," he says.

I am too frightened to speak.

"You'll need better clothes than that," he says, looking at my blue tunic and white blouse. He turns to Vater. "I will find her something good."

We walk back out, past the women and children with the yellow stars. I can feel more than one pair of eyes like heat on my back . . .

"What about this one?" said Ivan.

Gretchen . . .

I blinked once.

Gretchen Himmel. GH. My name was Gretchen Himmel.

I blinked again. I was back in the paint store with Ivan. I looked down at the colour he was pointing to. A pale buttery yellow. "No," I said. Yellow meant death. I could never sleep in a yellow room. I flipped the page so quickly that I nearly tore it.

"Careful," said Ivan, smoothing down the crease in the glossy paper.

My mind was still swirling between past and present. I clutched on to the side of the counter so I wouldn't fall.

Ivan looked at me strangely. "What's wrong, Nadia?"

I took a deep breath and tried to clear my thoughts. "I am fine," I said. I wanted to get this over with. "Let's look at some other colours."

Next was pinks and reds — everything from the palest blush of that long ago pink brocade dress to the violent red of blood. No, no, no.

The next page showed blues. My hand reached out of its own accord and touched a pale mauve. A wisp of scent tickled the edge of my brain. Lilac bushes in a much-loved garden.

"You'd like your room to be that colour?" Ivan asked. And I surprised myself. Yes, I did want that colour. Lilac would make me feel safe. I still wasn't happy about the thought of being closed up in a small room all night, but the colour would be soothing. And maybe I could convince Ivan to leave the door off.

He handed a lilac paint chip to the clerk and ordered one tin. We walked home, carrying the tin between us.

Ivan and I painted the room together. It didn't take long. It was a small room after all. But I still slept in the living room for the next few days to give the walls a chance to dry.

I was a bundle of nerves that first night in my own bedroom. But Ivan had found a second-hand lamp for me and he set it on the wooden crate that was my nightstand. "If you get scared, turn on the light," he whispered. He sat at the edge of my mattress and sang the *kolysanka* until I fell asleep. I dreamt of lilac bushes on a sunny, windy day . . .

Chapter Seven

School

I didn't see much of Marusia in those last weeks of summer. Some days she worked such long hours at the farm that she wouldn't get home until after dinnertime. The task of making an evening meal had fallen to me, but I didn't mind. I revelled in all the farm produce that Marusia would bring home, depending on the day or week — lettuce, cucumbers, corn, tomatoes, peaches, onions. In the camp, we ate rice, rice and more rice. Now our dinners were a big salad or corn, boiled potatoes and maybe a bit of sausage.

On the morning that I was to start school, Marusia woke me up early and said, "I have a surprise for you."

When she did it and how she found the time, I do not know, but she had made me a blouse and skirt from that bolt of blue cloth that one of the ladies had brought on our first day here. She had edged the collar with white hand-stitched daisies and had ironed smartly creased pleats into the skirt. I looked up at her through my tears.

"Put it on, *Sonechko*. You don't want to be late on your first day."

I slid my arms into the sleeves and as I did up each small white button, I noticed the delicate white stitches that circled each buttonhole. The skirt fit perfectly. Marusia gave me a new pair of white knee socks. Then, with a grin, she pulled out black shiny shoes from a paper bag. I tugged the socks up to my knees and then slipped my feet into the shoes.

"They're almost new," said Marusia. "I hope you like them."

I usually try to stay dignified with Marusia. She is not my mother, after all. But I felt the love she had put in every pleat and the affection of each stitch in this new blouse. I looked at the frayed corner of her own carefully pressed blouse and the lines of weariness under her smiling eyes. I scrambled onto her lap and hugged her fiercely. I could feel hot tears spilling down my cheeks.

"Nadia, my Nadia," Marusia said, drying my tears with the back of her hand. "I wanted to make you happy."

I tried to answer but I could not speak. I just nodded, hoping she realized how much I appreciated all that she did for me. I splashed cold water on my face to calm my swollen eyes, and then Marusia braided my hair.

Instead of doing it the usual way, she coiled it up like a crown and then topped it off with a huge white bow. I looked at myself in the mirror — seeing another me in another mirror. A younger me wearing a pink dress, my eyes red from crying . . .

"You look like you've seen a ghost," said Marusia.

I blinked. That younger me was gone like a wisp of smoke.

Marusia walked me to Central School. We were the first to arrive.

She pushed the door open and we stepped into the empty hallway. "Your room is down here," she said, tugging at my hand as she turned and walked down a corridor to the left. She knocked on the door, and when no one answered she turned the knob. The door opened. "Good luck," she said. She put her fingertips to her lips and blew a kiss to me as she walked out of the school. It wasn't until she was gone that I realized her walking me to school meant she had missed her ride to work.

I stepped inside the empty classroom. I had peered into this very classroom when I had taken my first walk around the neighbourhood. A large blackboard and a big desk were at the front. Rows of desks filled the rest of the room. Which one should I take? Would the teacher be upset if she came in and found me in the wrong place? I took a chance and sat in a desk in the back corner, then waited for the others to arrive.

In the camp, one of the men who had been a professor before the war taught the few older children a bit of history, and a woman who knew English held classes for the adults as well as children. We sat on benches and used our laps as desks. On the wall had been a paper poster of Taras Shevchenko, Ukraine's most famous poet. I don't know where the picture came from. I can't imagine anyone escaping the war with it. Maybe it arrived in a care package from Canada or the United States. I also had a vague recollection of lessons in German from a stern-faced woman in a one-room schoolhouse, but when this was I could not remember.

I looked down at the beautiful blue outfit that Marusia had made for me. I ran my fingers lightly over the fabric, loving that each stitch had been made just for me . . .

Vater in the drawing-room. An imposing figure in his black uniform. I see that his tall leather boots are covered with mud. No matter. There are slaves to clean up after him. He sets a package on top of the table and sits down. Mutter sits across from him, with her back rigid on the divan, a stiff smile on her lips. She pats the spot beside her. Eva scrambles to sit there. I sit beside Eva.

"This is for you, Gretchen," he says.

At first I am excited. I lean over and touch the brown paper lightly with one finger.

"Open it!" says Eva.

I look at her and see that she is almost bursting with excitement.

I pull the package to my lap and tear it open. A beautiful pink brocade dress. It is not like anything I have ever had before. I know I am supposed to be happy, but the sight of this dress makes me feel ill. I look up at Vater and put a smile on my face. "Thank you," I say.

Vater grins. "Now the entire Himmel family will look nice at the rallies."

I take it to my room. I hold it to my shoulders and turn to the mirror. I look like someone else.

That night, I cannot sleep. I turn on my bed lamp and get the dress. It smells of fresh laundry soap and a faint scent of something else. Sweat? I turn it inside out and examine it for clues. I notice an extra ribbon of cloth attached along the side of the back zipper. I fold it over. A name tag. Tiny embroidered letters: Rachel Goldstein.

A sudden image of that girl in the lineup, the one in yellow.

I push the dress away from me.

Children's voices coming through the classroom window, laughing and calling, sounding excited, yanked me back to the present. Tears welled in my eyes, so I took a deep breath and tried to calm myself.

I could tell from the sounds outside that other children were getting closer, but none of them came into the classroom. Maybe I should have waited outside instead of coming into this room? But just then a woman with straight hair cut to her chin walked in and I was trapped.

She smiled at me and said, "You must be our new student, Natalie Kraftchuk."

I stumbled to my feet and bowed my head to her and in my best English I said, "Good morning Mrs. Teacher. My name is Nadia Kravchuk."

She held out her hand to me. "I am Miss Ferris. The other children will be coming in soon."

I shook her hand. She turned and left the room, so I sat back down.

I heard a loud bell and nearly jumped back out of my seat. Within minutes, the hallway buzzed with children's voices. Miss Ferris came back into the classroom. Behind her was a line of children.

Chapter Eight

Humiliation

A gangly boy with short hair was the first to enter the classroom. He gazed around, then his eyes locked on mine. I could feel my embarrassment rising like heat as he stared at my shoes, my outfit, the bow in my hair. And then he laughed. I would have crawled under my desk if I could. He elbowed the boy who was coming in after him and pointed at me. That boy grinned. Next came a girl. She was dressed in a skirt and blouse, but nothing fancy. Her hair fell in loose curls to her shoulders. No bow. No braids. She glanced in my direction and then quickly looked away as if she hadn't seen me. She took a seat as far away from me as she could. Other students came in after her. Not one said hello and each scrambled to get a desk far away from me.

The last student to enter was a girl with golden skin and a glossy black braid that reached down almost to her waist. There was nowhere else to sit except beside me, so she did. She turned to me and smiled — she had a gap between her two front teeth and her eyes were friendly. "Hi," she said. "My name is Linda. What's yours?"

Linda. What a beautiful name. I could have cried from relief. "Nadia," I said. I wanted to ask if she lived in the neighbourhood, but I was such a bundle of nerves that the English words left me. Instead, I smiled stupidly at her.

"Children!" Miss Ferris stood at the front of the room and clapped her hands. "We have two new students this year. Natalie and Bob, please stand up."

Why was she calling me Natalie? I stumbled to my feet. A boy at the opposite side of the room also stood up, the tips of his ears turning red from the attention.

"Children, let us all welcome Natalie Kravchuk and Bob Landry."

"Welcome to Central School, Natalie and Bob," the students called out in ragged unison.

We both sat down. Bob's entire ears were now red, as was his face. I'm sure I was just as red. Miss Ferris took attendance and then passed out new workbooks and thick pencils. Then she had each of us stand up one by one and tell the class what we had done over the summer.

Because I was at the back of the class, my turn was last. That gave me time to prepare, but it also gave me time to get nervous. I had no idea how to explain what I did over the summer. I could do it in Ukrainian or Russian or Yiddish or German . . . but English? Finally it was my turn. I stood up.

"I am *Nadia* Kravchuk. I moved to Canada this summer," I said slowly and carefully.

There were rumblings of chuckles around me. I was about to sit down, but Miss Ferris said, "What did you do when you got here, Natal– Nadia?"

"I learned English."

One of the boys at the front of the class burst out laughing. "Not very well," he called out.

"Yeah," someone else said, "And she looks like a Nazi."

I could feel my face go hot with shame. My last name had been Himmel. I'd had a sister named Eva. I called my parents *Mutter* and *Vater*. Wasn't I a Nazi?

Marusia had told me again and again that I wasn't, but what about my memories? Her words and my memories didn't seem to match.

Miss Ferris rapped a ruler hard on her desk and shouted, "Silence!" She pointed at the two boys. "David and Eric, go to the principal's office. *Now*." I sat down, wishing I could disappear. It was bad enough that I looked and dressed differently from everyone else, but my accent made me stand out too.

I'm not quite sure what else she taught us that morning. All I could think about was getting home so I could change my clothes and comb out my hair. How I wished I could change my accent!

I dutifully copied down the things that Miss Ferris wrote on the board and I murmured thanks under my breath when she didn't call on me to say anything more. After what seemed like too many hours, a bell rang. I watched the others put their workbooks away. Thank goodness. My torture was over.

I closed up my books and shoved them into the desk and then followed the other students out the door. Linda, the one friendly student, was close behind me. As soon as the freshness of the outside air hit my face I felt a sense of relief. It had been like a prison in there. I began to walk out of the schoolyard and towards my house.

Linda trotted beside me and tugged on my arm. "You can't leave school property!"

I turned to her in confusion. The bell had rung, after all. "But the bell . . . "

Her mouth widened in its gap-toothed smile. "That was just the recess bell. You can't go home until the lunch bell."

"I cannot stay here."

"They'll send the truant officer after you!"

"The what?" I asked.

"The police. You can't go home during school."

Even the thought of police didn't stop me from leaving. Linda stood at the edge of the schoolyard with shock on her face, but I kept on going, picking up speed as I got farther from the school. The dressy shoes pinched at my heels, but I didn't slow down. By the time I got to our house I had a stitch in my side. I flipped the welcome mat at the front door and grabbed the key, opened the door and hurried in.

I had rarely been in the house alone and was struck by its eerie quiet. It was almost like the house was watching me with silent disapproval. I kicked off my shoes and ran upstairs, taking comfort in the sound of my feet thumping against the wooden steps. I threw myself onto the bed, punching my pillow in anger. How could I go back to that school? The other children hated me.

I shrieked at the top of my lungs and that felt good because only the house could hear me and I could be as miserable as I wanted. Once the tears began, they wouldn't stop. I cried out of pity for myself as the new kid at school. I cried in anger for feeling so helpless. But mostly I cried out of shame for the girl that I must have been in the past. Did I really belong here? Was I a Nazi? Maybe I didn't deserve to be safe. Where *did* I belong?

I don't know how long I cried, but my eyes got so puffy I could barely open them. I looked down at the beautiful outfit that Marusia had made me and realized that it was now wrinkled and damp. What an ungrateful, horrible person I was. How would Marusia feel about me now? Would she send me back to that other family, the one I had tried to push out of my memory?

I unbuttoned the blouse and tried to shake out the wrinkles. I hung it on a hanger and put it on the hook at the back of my door. I undid the skirt and stepped out of it, being careful not to damage it further. I folded it and smoothed out the wrinkles with my hands and then carefully set it in my top dresser drawer. I took out the oldest skirt and blouse that I could find and put that on instead. "It's all you deserve, you ungrateful thing."

It was *my* voice saying it, but it sounded like something I had heard long ago. I tried to undo my braids. I was able to get the elastics out from the bottom, but I couldn't undo the elaborate knot on the top of my head because Marusia had wrapped my braids together so tightly with the big white bow. My arms ached from the effort. I lay back down on the bed. I wanted to sleep, but couldn't, so I stared at the ceiling.

A scene from my past slid into my mind . . .

The men were separated from the women. I stood on my toes to see where they were going but it was too crowded. I thought of that girl in the yellow dress with the yellow star, standing in a lineup just like this.

"Remove all of your clothing," said a uniformed woman in a bored voice.

I turned to Marusia in alarm, but she was already unbuttoning her tattered and filthy blouse. She threw it on the pyramid of burning clothing. She took off her skirt and threw it in the fire as well. "Hurry, Nadia," she said.

My outfit had once been a pink party dress, but now it was blackened with grease and grass and sweat. How many flatcars had we ridden on and how many ditches had we hidden in to get to this place? The days blurred in my memory. I tried to undo my once-delicate ribbon belt, but it was shredded so badly that I couldn't find the beginning of the knot. And I couldn't reach the zipper at the back of the dress.

Marusia put her hands at the collar of my dress and with a single motion ripped it off me. She threw it into the fire.

"Undergarments too," said the woman.

We threw it all into the fire and then stood in the next line.

A woman with a large pair of shears cut off my braids, then snipped away until my scalp was bare. I watched my filthy hair fall onto the ground in clumps.

Marusia's face remained still as her hair was cut away. We stepped into line with the other refugees waiting for showers. At the door a woman sprayed us with something awful. I screamed.

"It will be all right," said Marusia. "That's just to kill the lice."

We crowded into the white-tiled room and were enveloped in scalding streams of water. I watched black trickles of grime and dead lice swirling down the floor drain.

I was glad to be free of that pink dress and all that it stood for. We were given sheets to cover our nakedness when we exited the shower. The sheets had lice, but we wrapped ourselves in them anyway.

Next came the interview. We stood in line yet again, shivering and damp, but cleaner than we had been since our escape. I stood on my toes to see what was happening at the front of the line. A uniformed man sat at a table, taking notes. He stamped a paper and sent the refugee in either one direction or another.

Marusia bent down and whispered in my ear. "Tell them you're my daughter. Your name is Nadia. You were born in Lviv . . . "

I knew that if they found out where I really came from, the Soviets would take me and I would be sent to Siberia. But where *did* I really come from? That I didn't know. Did Marusia?

A loud banging at the door snapped me back to the present. Linda had said it was against the law to run away from school. Were the police after me? I was too terrified to move.

Another banging. "Nadia!" A familiar woman's voice.

I peeked out the edge of my window. It was Miss Mac-Intosh. Maybe I could pretend that I wasn't home. But just as I was thinking that, she saw me. "Open the door!" she called. She didn't look happy.

I walked down the stairs, but still didn't open the door. I ran to the bathroom and looked at my face in the mirror. My eyelids were puffed out and red and my face was swollen. What would Miss MacIntosh think? I ran cold water over a cloth and held it to my face. The coolness was soothing, but when I looked back in the mirror, the same puffy eyes looked back at me. It was no use.

The knocking on the door was more insistent than ever now. "Nadia!" Miss MacIntosh called. "I know you're in there."

I opened the front door. The expression on Miss MacIntosh's face transformed in an instant from annoyance to concern. She stepped in and shut the door behind her.

"What has happened to you?"

I looked down at my feet and didn't answer. I was afraid that if I tried, it would be sobs, not words, that would come out.

All at once I felt Miss MacIntosh's warm arms envelop me and she picked me up like I was nothing more than a baby. She hugged me close and I felt myself go limp. I don't know whether it was relief or resignation. She carried me into the kitchen and sat down on a wooden chair, still holding me in her arms. She rocked me on her lap, even though my legs were almost as long as hers and my feet could touch the floor. She murmured, "It's going to be fine, Nadia."

I almost started to cry again, but something deep inside me told me that it was time to stop. So instead I took a deep breath and let it out slowly. I got myself out of Miss MacIntosh's arms, and stood up.

"Why are you here?" I asked.

"You ran away from school," she said. "You need to come back."

"I cannot." I folded my arms and tried to look defiant.

"You don't have a choice," said Miss MacIntosh. "It's against the law to run away from school."

So what Linda had told me was true. Would the police be coming next?

Miss MacIntosh must have noted the panic on my face. She said, "If you come back this afternoon, everything will be fine."

"But how can I go back, looking like this?"

"Be strong, Nadia," Miss MacIntosh said sternly. "I'm not even supposed to be here right now. I have yard duty. But when Linda told me you had run off, I had to check on you."

She stood up and opened our icebox. She took out two apples. "Hold these on your eyes. It will make the swelling go down."

As I did that, I could hear her making kitchen sounds — slicing bread and frying eggs. The aroma of sizzling butter and eggs made my stomach grumble. I heard a plate clatter onto the table.

"Eat," said Miss MacIntosh.

I took an apple off one eye. She was sitting across from me, eating an open-faced egg sandwich with a knife and fork. I set both apples down and devoured my own lunch. I was surprised at how hungry I was.

I took both plates to the sink and rinsed them when we were finished.

"We need to leave in fifteen minutes," said Miss MacIntosh. "I want to fix your hair."

We went into the bathroom together and I watched in the mirror as Miss MacIntosh carefully undid Marusia's elaborate braids from the top of my head. "It was a beautiful hairdo," she said. "Just not right for school."

As she combed out my hair, a strange expression appeared on her face. "You've got a black mark here," she said. "Right at the hairline."

I inhaled sharply. My tattoo. I turned my left palm upward and stared at the same mark on my inner wrist, but I turned it back down before Miss MacIntosh saw it. Both tattoos were so plain that most people didn't notice.

"It must be a mole," I lied.

I watched Miss MacIntosh's face in the mirror. She was about to say something, but then changed her mind. Sometimes I wondered if she knew more about my past than I did. She gently combed out the tangles. The comb in my hair reminded me of another woman who had tackled my tangles, but with the tug of resentment, not care. With it came another flicker of that pink brocade dress . . .

Miss MacIntosh didn't walk to school with me, which I was thankful for. She must have sensed how humiliating it was for me to go back at all, and arriving with a teacher would be that much more unbearable.

My eyes were still red from crying when I got back to school. The first bell had rung and students were just forming into lines. Some of the kids in my class looked up at me, then quickly turned away. Maybe Miss Ferris had said something to them. But then I heard Eric mutter, "The Hitler girl's back."

I stepped in behind Linda. "Good to see you!" she whispered.

I sat down in the same desk and tried to act as if nothing had happened. As Miss Ferris droned on with her lessons, I tried to sort out my recent memories. Why was it all coming back to me now? When we were in the DP camp, I just pushed my thoughts out of my mind. I tried that on the ship, and it mostly worked. But when we got to Brantford, the nightmares started up and the memories came back. Why wouldn't the sadness leave me alone?

Once we were all seated, I stared at the back of Eric's head a few seats in front of me. Why did he call me the Hitler girl? It was such a mean thing to do. I noticed that his brown hair was carefully trimmed short around the ears and was left a bit longer on top. He probably hadn't combed it since the morning, but it looked perfect. I was sure that it was a barber who had cut it, not a soldier. Had he ever had his hair hacked off for lice? Could he even imagine such a thing? How dare he judge me.

I looked up and down the rows of children in front of me. Each boy and girl looked well-fed and clean. No one was dressed in rags. They probably all had parents. My heart ached with jealousy. How I wished I lived a simple life that had never been touched by war.

Chapter Nine

Mychailo

I knew that Mychailo was the only other Ukrainian student at Central School, but I didn't see him until afternoon recess. He was tossing coins against a wall with some other boys and caught my eye. He nodded and went back to his game.

I saw him later walking home about a block behind me. I waited for him, but he was with some other boys. He walked right past me as if he didn't know me, so I walked the rest of the way home by myself.

Since I was the first one home, I began to peel some potatoes for supper. I had just filled a pot with water when there was a knock on the front door. It was Mychailo, a sheepish expression on his face.

"So, suddenly you know who I am?" I said.

"Come on," he said, shuffling his feet. "You didn't expect me to talk to you when I'm with a bunch of guys, did you?"

"I don't see why not." I left the door open, but walked back to the sink. He followed me in and sat down on a kitchen chair, watching me peel the potatoes.

"Want to go to the library?" he asked.

I did want to go to the library, but I was still angry, so I didn't answer.

"Are you going to cook them on low while we're gone?" he asked.

I shook my head, but still didn't say anything.

"You are going to go with me, aren't you?"

I liked that. It sounded a little like an apology. I finished peeling the last potato, rinsed them all off and put them in a pot of water. I didn't turn it on. Marusia had told me never to do that.

"I can go to the library for a short visit," I said. "I'll boil the potatoes when I get back."

Mychailo was silent for the first few minutes of our walk, then he said, "Sorry for not talking to you before."

I didn't say anything. I knew why he didn't talk to me. He didn't want to be teased. But it felt awful to have him treat me like a stranger.

When we got to the library, Mychailo went right to a trolley of books that were waiting to be re-shelved. "I discovered this a few days ago," he said. "All the best books are right here on this trolley." His eyes lit up as he pulled out a dog-eared novel called *Black Beauty*. "You'd like this," he said. "I read it last year."

I took it from him and flipped through it. All text and no pictures. And the text was small. "I can't read this," I said. He should have known. I had only taken out picture books so far.

"It will take you a while to read it," he said, "but I think you would like the story." He grinned at me then, and said, "It's a girly book."

"But you liked it."

He blushed a little bit at that, then shot back with, "It's got good action too."

He shuffled through the other books and found one on hockey, one on rocks, and another novel.

"What's the novel?" I asked, grabbing it out of his hand. It took me a bit to sound it out, and even once I did, I couldn't understand it. "*Freddy Goes to Florida*? What does *Freddy* mean?"

"Freddy," he said, "is a name, like Mychailo or Nadia. This particular Freddy is a talking pig."

"A talking *pig*?" That made no sense at all. "And what is *Florida*?"

"It's a place," he said, as if he couldn't understand my confusion.

"It doesn't make sense," I said. "Pigs don't talk and pigs don't go places unless they're taken by humans."

Mychailo rolled his eyes. "Maybe you should read one," he said. "Then you'd understand. They're hilarious. And *Freddy Goes to Florida* is the first in the series. I've been trying to borrow this one for quite a while."

"I bet you don't take those books to school with you."

"You're right about that," he said. "The hockey book is for taking to school."

I set *Black Beauty* down. It had too many words. "Can I try a Freddy book too?"

"Sure," said Mychailo. "Let's see if there are any on the shelf."

There were a few, so Mychailo drew out a copy of *Freddy the Detective*. "This was the first one I read," he said. "And it's really good."

I flipped through it. Even though it was a bit thicker than *Black Beauty*, the print was big and there were some pictures. Not quite a picture book, but not as daunting as *Black Beauty*. I breathed in deeply the wonderful scent of ink on paper and ran my hand across a page. Even the *feel* of this book made me happy . . .

I am in my four-poster bed in the German farmhouse. I should be asleep but I am woken by the rumble of voices from downstairs. I get out of bed. Shivering in my bare feet and thin nightgown, I slip down the stairs to see where the voices are coming from. The double doors of the library are open. Vater is seated with a brandy in one hand. Other men, their uniform jackets unbuttoned, sit around the table, telling each other stories and laughing. These are SS men. I know that because they have the very same badges on their collars as Vater.

But that is not what catches my eye. After all, I've seen them so often — at rallies in the city, and here for dinner parties. What I notice this time is the room they are in. It is usually closed. This room is lined from floor to ceiling with books, mostly in German, but some in other languages too. Fat books, thin books, some with gold lettering on their spines. I love books. I long to hold them. But I am not allowed to touch these books.

I walk back up to my room and pull out from under my bed the one book Vater has allowed me: Der Giftpiltz. I turn through the pages. The paintings are colourful and the print is large and clear. I want to love this book but I cannot. It talks about Jews and how they are poisonous toadstools but Germans are wholesome mushrooms. Something deep inside of me tells me this is wrong. I think of that girl who wore the yellow star and my heart aches. I close the book and shove it back under my bed.

"We should be going," said Mychailo. "Don't you have to put supper on?"

Suddenly I was back in the library in Canada. In Brantford. I looked at Mychailo, then up at the clock on the wall. We had been at the library for an hour.

We walked to the checkout counter, him with his three books and me with the one novel. I still felt a little bit like I was in a dream world.

An older boy who looked vaguely familiar from today's recess was standing in line in front of us. He turned, caught Mychailo's eye and nodded in greeting. He didn't seem to notice me, and that was fine with me. A few more people stood behind us in line. I didn't know most of them but recognized Linda. She was with a girl who was an older version of herself. It had to be her sister. Once my book was stamped, I waited for Linda and her sister to be checked through.

Mychailo tugged on my sleeve. "Come on," he said. "I thought you had to cook the potatoes."

"This will only take a minute." I knew he didn't want to be seen with me, but this wasn't a boy from school, it was two girls, so what was the harm? He stood impatiently by my side as Linda and her sister had their books stamped.

"Hi, Nadia," said Linda. She glanced at Mychailo, then back at me. "This is my sister, Grace."

Grace was taller than Linda, but she had the same chocolate-brown eyes and glossy hair. "So you are Nadia," she said, holding out her hand to me. "Good to meet you." She smiled at Mychailo, then tilted her head so she could read the spines of the books he was holding. "I didn't know you were a Freddy fan, Mychailo."

"You know each other?" I asked.

"Grace and I are in the same class."

Grace noticed the copy of *Freddy the Detective* in my hand. "How can *you* read *that*?"

I looked at her in surprise. What had Linda said about me to her sister? I knew my English wasn't perfect, but did she think I was stupid? "Slowly," I said, forcing my lips into a smile.

We stood chatting for a few minutes longer. "I've got to get home and turn on the potatoes before Marusia gets home," I said.

We walked up the half-flight of stairs together and out of the children's entrance. Linda and Grace walked with us as far as Sheridan Street, where Mychailo and I turned and they continued. Mychailo dropped his library books off at home and then we both went back to my place.

Once inside, I turned on the potatoes. Then we went out to the backyard and sat on the cinder blocks.

"You have to remember to call Marusia and Ivan your mother and father when you're talking to non-Ukrainians," said Mychailo.

My heart skipped a beat. "I always call them that."

Mychailo rolled his eyes. "You're so stupid you don't even know what you're saying."

I was about to yell at him, but I stopped. He was right. Didn't I just use Marusia's name with Linda and Grace? I would have to watch myself.

"Not everyone is perfect like you, Mr. Smarty-Pants," I replied.

"This is serious," said Mychailo. "I don't know where you really came from, but if you want to stay in Canada, you had better get used to calling Marusia and Ivan your mother and father."

I didn't say anything to that. I knew he was right and I was surprised at myself for slipping up. At the DP camp, I never let my guard down, but now that we were safely in Canada, my past was forcing itself to be remembered and my thoughts seemed to get all jumbled.

Just then we heard a truck stop in front of the house and Marusia's voice calling out a goodbye to the other farm workers.

"I should be heading home," said Mychailo. "Don't say hi to me at school, okay?"

I shrugged instead of answering. Maybe I would say hi to him just to get him angry.

A few seconds later Marusia came around to the back. She was carrying a heavy paper bag so I scooted over and grabbed it from her and we both walked inside.

She took the bag from my arms when we got inside and tipped it over onto the table, spilling out a few giant tomatoes, then onions, a small cabbage and some green peppers. At the bottom were half a dozen beautiful big apples. "I'll make apple squares for dessert," she said, her eyes sparkling.

She seemed to notice what I was wearing for the first time. "You've changed," she said.

Then she looked at my unbraided hair. "And you took your hair down."

We put the vegetables and some of the apples away in silence, and Marusia prodded the boiling potatoes with a fork to see how done they were. "How was your first day at school?" she asked.

I took a deep breath and held it. I needed to tell her right now what had happened. To clear the air and not hurt her feelings, but I couldn't get the words out.

Marusia's forehead crinkled in a frown, then she took a paring knife from the drawer and began to peel one of the apples. I watched the peel of apple skin grow. I had seen her skin an entire apple by paring off a single long tendril. Ivan couldn't do that. Neither could I.

The silence between us grew. I got the dishrag and wiped off the counter. I got out the broom and swept the floor even though it was already clean.

Marusia broke the silence. "I was telling the girls at the farm today about the outfit I made for you."

I didn't trust myself to say anything, so I caught her eye and tried to smile.

"They told me that students don't dress like that in Canada," she said. The apple was peeled, so she set it down on the counter and wiped her hands with a cloth. "Did you have trouble today?"

"I . . . I . . . love the new clothing." I stared at the floor and couldn't say any more. My throat was choked with tears.

Marusia stepped towards me, took the broom from my hands and set it against the wall. She held me tight. I exhaled. I could feel the tension and worry leave with that long-held breath. I rested my head on her chest and wrapped my arms around her waist, sinking into her warmth and the scent of apples, sweat and straw. I breathed in deeply, but I still couldn't speak.

She rocked me gently and murmured, "It's fine, Nadia. Don't worry. You're safe now, *Sonechko*."

The words soothed me. And with them came an image of another mother holding me and soothing me. Another time I thought I was safe . . .

That night in bed, I tried to remember more about the other time and another mother, but it was like trying to catch my shadow. I couldn't fall asleep, so I turned on my lamp, squinting at the sudden brightness. Once my eyes got used to it, I grabbed the Freddy novel and propped myself up on my pillow. On the cover was a pig wearing a cap, looking through a magnifying glass. Page one began, *It was hot* . . . That much I could read.

I tried to sound out more. The story seemed to be about two ducks looking at a house in the heat. It didn't make sense. Maybe if I wasn't so tired it would make sense. I set the book down and got *The Picture Dictionary for Children*. I had gone through the whole book four times, and each time I did I would find something new.

This time as I flipped through it, I kept on noticing the same couple of pictures that were used for various words. For example, the words *automobile*, *drives* and *parks* were all illustrated with a fancy car. It wasn't coloured in, but in my imagination, it was a shiny black car. The picture for *burn* was a house burning down, and the same burning house was used to show both *destroy* and *fire*.

My nostrils filled with the memory of smoke. How many times had I seen burning buildings? It was so familiar. Yet who was I and where was I when these things had happened? This was yet another piece of the puzzle that didn't fit.

I closed the book and waited for my heart to stop pounding. I didn't turn off the light.

I am in the back seat of a long black car, dressed in pink finery. The doors are locked and the windows rolled up tight.

I look out the window and through the haze of smoke. Girls and women running from a burning building. One girl glances my way. It is like looking into a mirror. She calls something to me but she's pushed away by a man in uniform. I pound at the window and pound at the door. Let me out, let me out!

The book slid off my chest and fell to the floor with a *thunk*. I jumped awake. The lamp was still on. I was safe in my bedroom in Canada. My head still swam with the nightmare. I rubbed my eyes and the image disappeared. I had been safe in the car and the fire was outside. Why had I wanted to get out? And who was that girl who looked like me? Was it just a trick of a dream, or did this really happen?

Chapter Ten

Linda

Those first few weeks of school were better than the horrible first day. Miss MacIntosh taught one of the higher grades and she'd nod to me when we passed in the hallway. Knowing she was in the building gave me comfort. It was the same with Mychailo. For all anyone could tell, we were strangers, but we were the only DP kids there and we had a special bond.

After school he would often drop by. He even helped me with homework once. If the other boys ever knew that, he would be teased. But I had Linda to play with at recess, and each day English seemed easier. I was grateful that Miss Ferris would not tolerate me being called "the Hitler girl" in her presence. But that didn't stop Eric and David from whispering it behind my back.

One recess as Linda and I were walking around the schoolyard pretending to be interested in watching the other children play, she turned to me and asked, "Would you like to come to my place after school today?"

I was delighted with the invitation, but had to say no. "Marus— Mama wouldn't know where I was," I told her.

"Can you come to my house instead?"

Linda grinned. "I could do that. I'll let Grace know and she can tell Mom and Dad where I am."

It felt nice walking all the way home with someone to talk to. Linda loved the swing Ivan had made for me. I showed her through the house as well. When I opened the doors to each of the rooms, I tried to see it through Linda's eyes. Would she think that we were extremely poor? What would she think of the chipped tub in the bathroom and the repainted icebox in the kitchen? She hadn't commented on the cinder blocks that we used as back-door steps, but I noticed her looking at them.

When we got up to my bedroom, she sat on the bed and tested the springs. "Comfy," she said. "And I love the lilac-coloured walls. Everything here is so fresh."

I looked at her face to see if she was making fun of me. I was sure that most of the kids at school had nicer homes than mine, but she seemed sincere.

"You must love it here," she said.

I was beginning to get used to my new home, and Canada was growing on me. Did I love it? Maybe. "The place I lived in before was much nicer than this," I said. The words were out before I knew it.

"Where was that?" asked Linda, flopping down on the bed.

"In Europe," I said, my heart starting to hammer. Why had I started this conversation?

"If you had a nicer place, why did you come here?"

I said nothing. I wished I could take back the words I had already let out.

"Doesn't make sense," said Linda.

"It was because of the war." I hoped that would end the conversation.

She looked at me strangely. "If you had a nicer place, were your parents well off?" she asked.

I opened my mouth to reply, but then closed it again. *Why* had I started this conversation?

"I was kidding," I told Linda. "We were just regular people."

Mychailo had warned me to never let Canadians know that Marusia and Ivan weren't my real parents, because the government could take me away from them. Marusia too, all those years at the camp, and on the ship.

I was so mad at myself for coming so close to betraying them. The last thing I wanted was to be separated from the only two people who had ever cared for me. I smiled at Linda and shrugged, hoping she'd brush off my comment.

"Nadia? I'm home!" The sound of the front door creaking open and Marusia's footsteps on the wooden entrance-way made me practically jump out of my skin.

"I'm up here," I called down. "With a friend."

I could hear Marusia walking into the kitchen on the level below us, and the rustling of a grocery bag as she set it on the table. Then I heard her footsteps on the stairs.

In a few seconds she appeared in the doorway of my bedroom. "There you are, Nadia." She looked from me to Linda. "Are you going to introduce me to your friend?"

"Ma— Mama, this is Linda. Linda, this is my mother."

Linda scrambled to her feet and held out her hand. "Glad to meet you, Mrs. Kravchuk."

Marusia shook Linda's hand. "Come on downstairs in

a couple of minutes. I'll go make you a treat." She turned and walked back down the stairs.

When we could hear her down in the kitchen again, Linda whispered to me. "What did she do in the war?"

I didn't know how to answer that. Why hadn't I been quiet about it like Mychailo had warned me to? "I'll tell you about it later. Let's go get our snack," I said, hoping she would forget about all of this.

When we went downstairs, Marusia had sliced an apple in a bowl for each of us and drizzled them both with honey. "You can take it outside to eat if you like," she said. "But bring the bowls back when you're finished."

The swing was just wide enough to hold us both if we squeezed on together, and Linda's legs were long enough to keep it steady, so that's where we sat together and ate our snack.

"This is yummy," said Linda, crunching with satisfaction.

I loved the gooey treat too. It wasn't something Marusia had ever made just for us. I guess she wanted to serve something special for my friend. She always tried so hard to make things good for me. It made me feel guilty for the things I had said to Linda.

Linda looked over to the house and whispered to me. "She can't hear us from inside, can she?"

"I don't think so."

"So what did she do during the war?"

I slowly swallowed the piece of apple that sat on my tongue. "I was just being silly." I said. "She was a factory worker."

"What about you?" asked Linda. "It must have been

exciting to grow up in the middle of a war."

Exciting? I had never thought of it that way. So terrifying that I couldn't remember half of it, that's what it was to me. "I was young," I said. "It's all jumbled in my mind."

"Tell me what you remember, then."

So I told her about Marusia and I escaping and our arrival at the Displaced Persons' camp. Linda's eyes went wide as I told her some things. I held back the ones about the German family.

The back door opened and Marusia stuck her head out. "You two are cosy on that swing," she said, grinning. "Finish up your apples. Linda, Nadia and I will walk you home."

"I can walk home myself," said Linda.

"We would like to walk you home," said Marusia.

She washed and shone some apples and put them in a paper bag to take with us. I was puzzled at first, but then realized what Marusia was up to. She wanted to meet Linda's parents. The apples were a gift.

Linda's one-storey yellow brick house was on Usher Street — behind the railway station and one street closer than the Ukrainian church. I had passed by on the way to church, but never realized she lived there.

"Would you like to come in?" Linda asked.

"That's not necessary," said Marusia. "I just wanted to make sure that you got home safe."

Linda knew as well as I did that the real reason for this little walk home was to check out her family. "Wait here," she said. "I want my mom to meet you."

She ran ahead of us and flew in the front door of her house. A moment later a careworn woman drying her hands on a blue apron stepped out onto the front step and greeted us, Linda peeking out from behind her. "I'm Rita Henhawk, Linda's mother."

"I'm Marusia Kravchuk, and this is my daughter Nadia. Here are some apples," she added, holding the bag out to Mrs. Henhawk. "I picked them today."

Mrs. Henhawk took the bag and smiled. "Are they from your own tree?"

"No," said Marusia. "I work at a farm."

Mrs. Henhawk nodded in understanding. "Can you come in for a cup of tea?" She opened the door wide. A striped cat darted between her legs and ran out onto the road.

I was about to chase after him, but Linda's mother said, "Don't worry. He'll be back. Joe never misses his supper."

We stepped inside the house and were enveloped by warmth and a savoury scent of something cooking. "Excuse the mess," said Mrs. Henhawk. "I've been making corn cakes."

There was no mess. The front door led directly into a living room that had only a few pieces of furniture in it. They had a worn sofa, two hardback chairs and a wooden chest that served as a coffee table. There were no bookshelves and the wooden floor was bare, but it was a tidy room. I could tell that the Henhawks were poor, but proud like us. So Linda had been sincere about the nice things she'd said about our house. That made me feel so much better.

Beyond that was a kitchen with a red linoleum floor, so newly mopped it was still glistening. A carved wooden bowl covered with a checkered cloth sat on one end of the kitchen table. Linda's older sister sat on a chair at the opposite side of the table, a textbook and binder spread out before her and a half-finished glass of milk close at hand. Grace looked up when we stepped in, gave a bit of a wave and went back to her homework.

"Make yourselves comfortable," Mrs. Henhawk said, indicating the sofa. "I'll put the kettle on."

"That would be lovely," said Marusia. She sat down on the sofa and patted the spot beside her. I sat down.

"And some milk for you, young lady?" Mrs. Henhawk asked me.

I wasn't thirsty, but Marusia nudged me in the ribs, so I said that would be lovely. Linda went into the kitchen to help. In a few moments she came back out, carrying two glasses of milk and two mugs of tea on a tray. Her mother came out of the kitchen with a platter of small golden cakes.

I held my corn cake in both of my hands and blew on it to cool it down. Marusia took a bite of hers. Smacking her lips with delight, she said, "This is delicious."

I bit into mine and had to agree. It was like butter, corn and bacon all mixed together.

"It's an old family recipe," said Mrs. Henhawk. "I'm glad you like them."

Marusia and Mrs. Henhawk made small talk while Linda and I sat impatiently waiting for them to finish. I would have liked to explore the neighbourhood with Linda. Or at least explore the house. But I knew this step was necessary. Marusia is very protective of me.

Finally, Marusia finished her tea and set down the cup. "It was so good to meet you," she said. We both stood.

"They seem like nice people," said Marusia, as we walked back home. "You can go there after school sometimes, but you've got to let me know the day before."

Chapter Eleven

Ghosts

I had a friend in Linda, parents who loved me and a roof over my head. The weeks marched by, and before the first frost, Ivan had finished all the painting and had installed the inside doors. Marusia and I planted tulip and daffodil bulbs by the front walk. I looked forward to seeing them bloom the following spring. I was lucky to be loved by Marusia and Ivan.

It wasn't all perfect. Eric still called me "the Hitler girl" whenever he saw me at recess or on the way home — and he made a point of seeing me often. Thank goodness that other boy had tired of the game. My memories of the past had stopped coming at me so quickly and I was able to sort some of them out, but there were still huge blanks in my memory.

On the last Sunday evening in October, I sat between Marusia and Ivan on the cinder-block steps at the back of our house. Someone in the neighbourhood must have been burning leaves, because there was a haze in the air and I could smell smoke. Marusia brewed a pot of camomile tea with honey and we each sipped a mug of it.

As I sat there between the two people who had changed their lives to protect me, I looked at the swing that Ivan had made me. I saw the lilac bushes that he had planted for me. I thought of Marusia protecting me in the camp and of the skirt and blouse that her farm-worn hands had stitched with love. I began to cry.

"*Sonechko*," said Marusia, leaning her head onto my shoulder. "What is the matter?"

My throat was filled with sobs. "Nothing . . . it's fine, it's fine . . . " I tried to stop the tears but they had a mind of their own.

"Did you have another nightmare?" asked Ivan.

I shook my head. "I am happy," I said. "I don't know how you can love me, but I'm glad that you do . . . "

"Nadia, Nadia," cooed Marusia. "You may not be the daughter of my blood, but you are the daughter of my heart. I love you and Ivan loves you."

"But I don't deserve to be loved," I sobbed. "You say I'm not a Nazi, but my memories say I am."

Ivan pulled a handkerchief out of his pocket and dried my tears. "Tell us everything you know, Nadia. Maybe we can help you make sense of it all."

My memories tumbled out. I told them about Eva and the pink dress and where I thought it came from. I told them about the books I was forbidden to read and the one I was forced to read. I told them about meeting Hitler. It seemed like Marusia had known some of this, but not all. Ivan sat listening in silence, his lips set in a thin grim line. When I finished, I was empty of tears.

"Do you remember when we met?" Marusia asked.

I closed my eyes and thought hard. Marusia was so

much a part of my life, but *exactly* when we met? I drew
a blank. Marusia and I escaping on the flatbed of the train
was a vivid memory. And the day we arrived at the DP
camp. On the edge of my dreams was an image of
Marusia with that same German family at that same farm
in the countryside. I didn't know how she fit in, but she
was somehow there and so were lilac bushes. Marusia
back then was like a once familiar song now forgotten.

"Do you want me to tell you about it?" she asked.

I began to shake. I had no idea why. "Not now."

Marusia lightly touched my forearm with her fingers. "I
don't mean to push you," she said. "But it is important for
you to fill those forgotten parts of your life. Otherwise,
we'll never find out who you really are."

That is what scared me the most. Did I *want* to know
who I really was? What if I didn't like that person? That
was the thought I fell asleep to . . .

*I pull at the handle of the door but it won't open and the
window won't roll down. I pound on the glass. "Let me out,
let me out." Outside, the world is filled with smoke. I hear
sirens. See a face that looks like mine.*

The front door clicked softly open and shut. I bolted
out of bed and scrambled to the window. Ivan. I knew it
was Ivan on his way to the foundry in the darkness of the
early morning. Why did this sound scare me so?

I rubbed the sleep out of my eyes and thought of the
dream that was still a fragment of fear in my mind. Why
did I dream I was trying to get out of a safe car when a
building was burning outside? It made no sense. And
how could I be outside and inside that car at the same
time?

I tiptoed downstairs and slipped out to the backyard. I sat on my swing in the darkness and breathed in the faint scent of burned leaves. The smell reminded me of something that happened long ago, something I *did* remember . . .

The long black car idled beside the smoking ruin of a newly bombed factory. Vater got out. "I won't be long," he said to Mutter as he closed the door.

"You'd better not be," Mutter said, more to herself than to Eva or me. "We can't be late for this rally."

Yet another rally. It was hot in the car and my pink dress felt itchy. My hair was pulled so tightly into a braid that my scalp ached. Eva's hair cascaded loose down her back and her dress was made of cool pink muslin, yet she couldn't sit still. The buckle of her shoe nearly caught on my skirt as she clambered over me to get to the window. I smoothed it back down and sighed.

"Sit down, Eva," said Mutter, reaching over me to tug at Eva's dress, but Eva stayed where she was.

"It's hot in here, Mutti." Eva rolled down the window and a cool smoky breeze drifted in.

"We're going to smell like smoke," said Mutter.

"At least we won't smell sweaty," said Eva.

Had I said that, I would have been slapped. I arched my neck so I could see what was happening at the factory. I knew that this one made weapons for the war and that was why it was attacked.

One long wing of the building was bombed flat and smoke curled out of the remains. Anyone who had worked in that part of the factory would have died.

Vater was giving orders to boys who wore swastika armbands. Frightened women in grey rags limped out of billowing smoke. Everything was in shades of grey except for the slashes of blood on clothing where sharp fragments of blasted brick had cut forearms and shoulders. Blood dried a sticky brown in tangles of blond and black and chestnut hair where shrapnel had hit scalps.

"Why aren't they wearing the yellow stars?" asked Eva.

Mutter leaned over to get a better look at the women. I did the same. These ones were wearing white and blue badges saying OST.

"They're the eastern workers," said Mutter.

"Are they animals like the Jews, Mutti?"

"Yes, dear, that's why they work in the munitions factory. You wouldn't want Germans to get bombed, would you?"

I squinted at individual faces in the sad and tattered crowd of OST workers. One girl had hair not quite as fair as my own. As if she could feel my stare, she looked up. It was like I was seeing an older version of myself. Our eyes met and her mouth formed a wide O of shock. She tried to call something to me but then one of the Hitler Youth stepped in front of her and pushed her away . . .

The back door opened with a squeak. I blinked once, and then again, and looked around. It was daylight and I was on my swing. My feet were blue with cold. I looked to the back door and Marusia was standing there, clutching a thin housecoat around her shoulders.

"Nadia," she said. "I had no idea you were out here. You are going to catch your death."

I stumbled a bit on frozen legs as I got off the swing. Marusia wrapped a blanket around me when I got inside. She busied herself at the stove, then set a mug of scalding cocoa on the table in front of me. It warmed my fingers as I raised it to my lips. Flashes and flakes of that memory still seemed as real as my cocoa. That girl who looked like me — I knew now that it wasn't me. And the OST badge she wore — where had I seen one before?

"Did you remember something more?"

"Not about when we met," I said. "I remembered about that black car and I know why there was smoke."

I told her about the bombing and the girl who looked like me. She reached out and took one of my hands. She didn't say anything for a bit. It was like she was trying to figure out what to say. "Millions from Ukraine and Poland were taken as *Osturbeiters* — OST workers."

I had an image of Marusia in a worn grey dress, with an OST badge stitched to her chest. I set my cocoa down so quickly that some of it sloshed onto the table. I covered my face with my hands, but the image wouldn't go away. "You were an OST worker too, weren't you?"

"Nadia," Marusia said. "Your memory is coming back. Do you remember when we met?"

"Were you at that bombed-out factory? Was it you I saw?" But even as I asked the question, I knew that I was wrong. Looking at Marusia was not like looking at an older me.

"We met at the farm, Nadia. Try to remember."

Parts of it came back to me . . . The military truck stopping in our drive. A soldier unlatching the back door and an OST woman tumbling out onto the gravel. From the stench I could tell she'd been travelling for a long time. Marusia trying to stand, but her legs so wobbly that she fell back down. Looking up and seeing me. Then me feeling so guilty of my finery and of who I was, and running back into the farmhouse to hide in shame.

"I remember, Marusia," I said in a small voice. "I remember now. Where did you come from?"

"Zelena," said Marusia. "A small village in eastern Ukraine. The Germans came and ordered everyone my age to come to the village square. Anyone who didn't come was rooted out and shot. They sorted through us. I was loaded into the back of a truck." She brushed a tear from her cheek with the back of her hand. "It wasn't heated and we weren't given food. Some people had bits of food with them and we shared it. We travelled for many days."

"And then you were taken to the farm?"

"No," said Marusia. "I was sent to work at the Ford Werke factory in Cologne."

Wisps of the past drifted into my mind. The bombed-out weapons plant . . . "I'm glad they didn't have you making bombs," I whispered.

"In that way I was lucky," said Marusia. "But we were still slaves."

"How did you get to the farm?" I asked.

"At the car factory, they locked us into a big barracks at night," said Marusia. "But I escaped. I was caught and sent back, but the factory didn't want me back. They said I was undependable, so I was sent to a concentration camp. But I convinced them that I was a good cook. I was given to General Himmel, who gave me to his wife."

I stared at my cocoa. The man that I knew as Vater, Marusia knew as General Himmel. The thought of what she had been through made my stomach churn.

"It is good that you're beginning to remember," she said. "As you remember more, you will understand why you have nothing to feel guilty about."

"Why don't you just tell me everything you know about my past?" I asked her. "Wouldn't that be simpler?"

"I don't know your whole past," said Marusia. "I'm afraid that if I tell you what I know, it could influence your memories. It's best for you to air this out as the memories surface."

"That's easy for you to say," I told her angrily. "You don't have to live with these nightmares."

Marusia was silent for a moment. She brushed away a tear from her eye, then reached out her hand and placed it on top of mine. "I am living with my own ghosts, *Sonechko*."

Chapter Twelve

Red Ink

At school later that morning, I tried to pay attention, but as Miss Ferris wrote notes on the board, the words seemed to blur and blend together. I kept on thinking about that girl who looked like an older me. Who was she and why did she appear in my nightmares? I was so absent-minded that I didn't hear the bell for morning recess. Linda touched my arm and I nearly jumped out of my seat.

"Sorry!" she said. "You look like you've seen a ghost."

I blinked a couple of times to try to clear the images from my mind. Maybe that girl who looked like me was just a ghost of my imagination? "Let's go outside," I said.

Linda sped down the hallway in front of me and pushed open the door. I followed her on legs that felt like rubber.

"You're acting strange today," said Linda, once we were outside.

"Sorry," I said. "I don't feel very well."

"Maybe the fresh air will do you some good."

Except the air wasn't fresh. It smelled of burning leaves. We walked past a group of girls from our class who were clustered together chatting quietly. I overheard bits of their conversation. Hallowe'en was tomorrow and they were talking about what costumes they would be wearing for the class party — a witch, a ghost, a nurse . . .

Others were playing double dutch with the younger students, but none of them called to Linda or me to ask us to join. Most of the boys were out in the field tossing around a football. How I wished that I could be like these other students. Wouldn't it be wonderful to not have a past?

When we got back into the classroom, I noticed an envelope sticking out of the corner of my workbook. I had a moment of panic. Had Miss Ferris noticed that I wasn't paying attention this morning? Maybe it was a note sending me to the principal's office. I pulled the envelope out of my workbook and breathed a sigh of relief. A big childish N was written on the front in red ink and the writing didn't look at all like Miss Ferris's tidy script. Could this be an invitation to a birthday or Hallowe'en party? I looked over to Linda's desk. There was no envelope on hers. I couldn't possibly go to a party if she hadn't also been invited.

Most of the other students had returned to their desks by this time but class hadn't begun and Miss Ferris still sat at her desk at the front of the room, marking papers. I held the envelope on my lap so Miss Ferris wouldn't see me opening it. I ripped it open as quietly as I could and pulled out the piece of paper — a crude drawing of girl with yellow braids — covered in red swastikas. Underneath, someone had written, *Nazi Nadia, go back to Hitler-land!*

"Nadia, what are you reading?" Miss Ferris asked in a

sharp voice. She stood at the front of the room with her hands on her hips. "You know we don't pass notes in class."

I shoved the paper into my desk, but the envelope fluttered to the floor. Several of my classmates turned to watch me. Eric was grinning and David covered his mouth to keep from laughing out loud.

"Noth– nothing . . ." I said. "I was just getting out my workbook."

"Your workbook is on your desk," said Miss Ferris sternly. "Stand up, and share with us what you find so interesting."

I stumbled to my feet, but didn't take the horrible note out of my desk. I could feel my heart pound in my chest. How could I possibly read it out loud?

"Get the note, Nadia. We would all like to hear it."

I stood there, frozen. Miss Ferris marched down the aisle and knelt at my desk. She pulled the offending piece of paper out and unfolded it.

Her face became still. "Sit down, Nadia," she said, resting her hand gently on my shoulder. She walked to the front of the classroom and held up the hideous drawing for everyone to see. A hush fell over the room. Someone giggled. I crouched down in my seat. If only I could disappear.

"Who did this?" she almost shouted. No one raised a hand. "You will all have a detention if the guilty party does not step forward."

This time she did shout. No one raised their hand. I stared at the back of Eric's head. He sat rigid, with his hands folded neatly on his desk. I was sure he was no longer grinning. I couldn't be sure if it was him or David. It could have been anyone. I felt embarrassed and small.

"Hands on your desks, everyone," Miss Ferris said sternly. "Palms up." She marched up one aisle and down the next, examining everyone's hands for red ink. When she got to David's desk she stopped. She grabbed one of his hands and twisted it back and forth. "Red ink," she said. "Empty your desk. Now!" David reached into his desk and emptied it of books and notebooks and pens and pencils. Miss Ferris looked through each item carefully for more evidence and then tossed it to the floor.

"That's all I have," he said with an innocent look on his face. Miss Ferris reached inside his desk and rooted around. She pulled out a pad of paper and a fountain pen filled with red ink. She flipped through the paper. More sickening sketches of "Nazi Nadia." I crouched farther down in my seat.

"Get up," said Miss Ferris. She grabbed David by the ear and marched him out of the room. Once the door slammed shut behind them, a couple dozen pairs of eyes turned to stare at me.

I convinced Marusia and Ivan to let me stay home from school on Hallowe'en. I did not feel like dressing up in a silly costume and pretending that I was having fun just a day after David's nastiness. Doing chores around the house was preferable. "Let us not make this a habit," Marusia warned me.

I was at the kitchen sink scrubbing grass stains out of one of her work shirts when I spied Mychailo at the back door. He wasn't wearing a costume. "It's open," I called through the window. "Didn't your class have a party this afternoon?" I asked him as he stepped inside.

"We did," said Mychailo. "I just put a sheet over my head and called myself a ghost."

That made me smile.

He rooted through his pockets and pulled out a candy kiss. "Here," he said, holding it out for me. "Now you can say you've been kissed by a boy."

That made me blush. "Thanks," I said. "Put it on the table." My hands were still soapy. I rinsed Marusia's shirt, wrung it out and then hung it on the laundry line outside. I opened up the candy kiss and popped it into my mouth.

"Are you going trick or treating tonight?" Mychailo asked. "You can go with me if you want."

I hadn't planned on going trick or treating. After the incident at school yesterday, I didn't even feel like going outside. The whole thing was so shameful. Besides, this custom of Hallowe'en seemed strange to me — and a little bit scary. "I don't have a costume."

"You can go as a ghost," he said. "Or a hobo." He looked at me with impatience. "Those costumes are easy. Don't you want free candy?"

I had to admit that the thought of free candy was exciting. And if I did go trick or treating, I would feel safe going with Mychailo. "I'll ask Mar— *Mama* and *Tato* if I can go," I said.

"Great," he said. "I'll come by just as it starts to get dark."

❖ ❖ ❖

Ivan was pleased that I had decided to go out trick or treating and he was especially happy that I was going with Mychailo. "You need to be a child more often," he said.

And he helped me put together a costume. I was a scarecrow, with itchy long grass from the far edges of the backyard stuffed in a flannel shirt of Ivan's. On top, I wore a pair of Marusia's overalls that were so old they were patched on the patches. Ivan used her red lipstick to paint on a scarecrow face. We had no candy to give out, but we did have a bowl of apples from Marusia's farm that she had polished to a glossy sheen.

I could tell by the expression in Marusia's eyes that she was less sure about me going out, but she pretended to be happy. She gave me an extra-long hug goodbye when I left with Mychailo. "Stay on this street," she said. "And be home in an hour."

One nice thing about living on a street with close-together houses is you can get to a lot of them in an hour. My pillowcase was soon full of treats: candy apples and caramel corn, bubble gum and peanuts. I dumped all of my candy out on the kitchen table when I got home. Ivan, Marusia and I ate far too much of it. I went to bed with a stomach ache. I tossed and turned all night and had a long and scary dream. In the morning I could only remember bits and snatches.

Chapter Thirteen

Mansion

I got into the habit of going to Linda's house on Tuesdays after school and she came to my house on Thursdays. It was hard to find a place to play inside. Linda shared a bedroom with Grace on the second floor. They had bunk beds and a bookshelf crammed with old novels. I longed to look through that bookshelf, but the bedroom itself made me feel like I couldn't breathe. I think part of it was because Grace was always there. She'd either be reading, propped up on a pillow on the top bunk, or she'd have a friend over and they'd be doing a project for school or something.

There wasn't much of a place to play in Linda's backyard either. It was nothing more than an overgrown strip of land on a hill with wild bushes along either side and a laundry line down the middle. Linda had a deck of cards and we tended to play Crazy Eights or Concentration at the kitchen table, but then one Tuesday she brought out a board game called Monopoly.

With the cards, we could play several games in the space of an hour or two, but Monopoly was a much longer game. Marusia would get dropped off at Linda's house on Tuesdays after finishing at the farm, but once we started playing Monopoly, the game would just be getting interesting when Marusia would arrive and it was time for me to leave.

"Can you come to my house on Saturday?" asked Linda. "Mom said you could stay even if the game takes all day."

Marusia and Ivan agreed. Linda's mother suggested I come early on Saturday morning and she invited me to stay for lunch. Ivan was doing some yardwork at the Ukrainian church, so he walked me to Linda's house, and we decided that once I was finished, I would walk over to the church to meet him and we'd walk home together.

When I got to Linda's, it was just before nine. Mrs. Henhawk was in the kitchen making applesauce. "Linda will be down in a minute," she said. She offered me an apple, but I had just eaten breakfast.

"Take a seat beside George." She pointed to the chair beside her husband. "He won't bite."

I sat down and Mr. Henhawk lowered his newspaper, caught my eye and gave me a wink. He seemed as friendly as Mrs. Henhawk was.

I must have let a fly into the house when I came in through the back door. It kept buzzing around my head. I waved it away but it kept coming back. Suddenly, I felt a whack of a newspaper against the side of my head.

I blinked once and then again. Why would Mr. Henhawk hit me like that? I barely heard what he was saying to me now . . .

"Don't stuff yourself, Eva," Mutter is saying as she tries to pull the plate away, but Eva grabs it with two hands and pulls it back.

"They're my favourite, Mutti, and you know it," says Eva, cutting off a giant portion of apple-filled Eierkuchen *and shoving it into her mouth. A chunk of apple falls out and lands on the table. She picks it up and pops it back into her mouth.*

"If only that one would eat half as much as you." Mutter looks at me. "If the führer *hears we've starved his little darling, it will be the end of us."*

I look at the plate in front of me and pick up my knife and fork. I cut one bite and hold a piece of Eierkuchen *to my mouth, but the greasy smell of it makes me feel sick. I think of the women and children with the yellow stars. How can I eat this when it seems they have nothing? I push the plate away.*

Mutter slaps me hard across the face.

"Nadia, are you all right?"

Mr. Henhawk's voice pulled me back to the present. I was standing by the table in the Henhawk kitchen, a chair upended beside me. I lifted my hand to my cheek. I could almost feel the tingle of that long ago slap from Mutter.

"I'm fine," I told him.

But I didn't feel fine. These scenes from the past made me queasy and confused.

Linda appeared in the kitchen doorway holding the Monopoly box. "Nadia, you don't look so good."

The kitchen was humid, with an overwhelming smell of apples. I felt like I was going to be sick. "Would you mind if we played outside instead?" I asked.

"Sure," said Linda. She set the Monopoly box on the kitchen table. "We'll be outside, okay?" she said to her parents.

"Stay in the neighbourhood," said Mr. Henhawk.

I gulped in fresh air as we stepped out to Linda's narrow, overgrown backyard.

"Let's go to the park," she said.

I didn't know that there was a park. I walked beside Linda as she stayed on her own side of Usher Street and headed west. As we got farther from where she lived, I noticed that the houses seemed to get shabbier. Usher curved into Rushton Street and I noticed a fancy wrought-iron gate almost hidden by bushes. It looked like something from a storybook. Was I dreaming, or was this real? I went up to touch the gate.

"Come this way and I'll show you something better," said Linda, grabbing my hand.

So it was real.

We walked around the curve. Through the bushes I could see that the gate was attached to a long fancy fence, also almost completely hidden by leaves. But all at once there was a break in the bushes. I was so shocked by what I saw that I grabbed Linda's shoulder to steady myself. A rundown mansion on top of a hill. It seemed out of time and place, like something from a dream — or a nightmare. It felt a little sinister, with paint peeling from the latticework and ragged curtains hanging limp inside shattered windows.

"That's Yates Castle," said Linda. "I don't think anyone lives there anymore, except maybe hobos."

Something about the vast abandoned mansion tugged

at my memory, but why? It looked nothing like the large, well-kept farmhouse I had lived in with Eva and Mutter and Vater. And there was no building like this in the DP camp, of course. Hot bile rose up in my throat and I doubled over, gagging.

"Nadia, are you all right?" asked Linda.

I took a few heaving breaths and tried to calm myself. After a couple of minutes I was able to stand up straight again. "I'm — fine," I managed.

"What's wrong? Does the house scare you?" she asked.

I couldn't answer.

"Does it remind you of something during the war?"

"It must," I told her. "But I don't know what."

"Come on," she said, grabbing my hand again. "Let's get away from here."

As we walked past the mansion — or castle or haunted house, whatever it was — I couldn't tear my eyes from it. It was awful and beautiful at the same time . . .

I am being carried, kicking, screaming, up white-painted steps. "Baba! Baba! I want my baba!" I am put in a room all by myself. I try to open the door but it's locked. I pound until my knuckles bleed but no one answers.

Linda was saying my name, but I ran down the block, pulling her with me. I had no idea where I was going but I had to get away from that house.

"Slow down!" she cried, tugging on my hand. "I've got a stitch in my side."

When I stopped running, I realized that I was huffing for breath and covered in sweat. I felt Linda's hand take mine and she led me up a pathway through the trees. We stepped out onto tidy grass on a hill. It was open and airy and not scary at all. It was hard to believe that such a nice park was hidden from anyone strolling down Usher Street.

She led me to the middle of the open space and we both flopped onto the grass. For long minutes, we lay there side by side, watching the clouds and not saying a word.

Then Linda asked, "What did Yates Castle remind you of?"

A feeling of dread came over me. I sat up and looked at Linda. I had confided some things about my other past to her already. I longed to talk to her about those scenes that would flash into my mind. But would she understand? More importantly, would she tell anyone else? Mychailo had warned me about talking to Canadians. But Linda was my best friend, after all. I had to tell her something.

"All I remember is being locked up in a fancy house," I said. "That, and how frightened I was."

"Who would have locked you up?" she asked, a puzzled expression on her face.

"I don't know."

"Was it your parents?"

"No!" It was hard to even think of Marusia or Ivan doing anything like that to me.

I didn't say anything more, so Linda dropped the subject. We played a few games, like I Spy, and finding shapes in clouds, and then she said we should go to the church to find Ivan. "After the scare you've had, I'm sure you want to go home."

I looked at Linda with new appreciation. What a kind friend she was.

"Do we have to go past that house again?" I asked her.

"We don't have to," she said. She pointed up the hill. "That's Terrace Hill Street. We can go up that way to your church."

"Are you sure you don't mind us not playing Monopoly?"

"Nadia," said Linda. "Of course I don't mind. We can always play another day."

Once we got up the incline to Terrace Hill Street, we had a beautiful view of the train station and beyond. You could see almost all the way to my house, yet the castle was hidden by trees.

As we walked down Terrace Hill Street, I was surprised at how close the Ukrainian church was, and I was disturbed to realize that Yates Castle and the church were actually back to back. In fact, along the side of the church and extending down to the castle was a set of steps and a carriage road. My heart tightened. That little church had been one of the few places I had felt truly safe, but now that I realized how close it was to that creepy house, I wondered if the church would ever feel like a safe place again.

Ivan was raking the leaves off the lawn in front of the church. I noticed that Mychailo was helping his father plant a row of shrubs along the church walkway. When we got there, Ivan looked at me with surprise. "You're finished your game already?"

"We're not finished, but . . . " I looked to Linda.

She caught my eye and nodded. "We got bored," she said, shrugging. "We'll play another day."

Ivan looked at the pile of leaves he had raked up and then gazed at the rest of the lawn. "I won't be finished here for at least another hour."

"I could help you," I said

"So could I," said Linda. "Do you have any more rakes?"

I looked at her and smiled in thanks.

Ivan grinned. "It won't take long at all with three of us working."

When we were finished with the yardwork, Ivan took my hand and began to walk towards those dreaded steps that led down to Usher Street alongside Yates Castle.

"This is a quick way to Linda's," he said. "And I want to show you an interesting house."

Ivan knew about it! Of course he did. He had been doing yardwork at the church. How could he miss seeing a castle behind the church? I was just surprised that I had never noticed it through the trees before.

I didn't budge from my spot on the sidewalk. "That place scares me."

Ivan's forehead crinkled in surprise. He looked at me, then at Linda. She shrugged her shoulders. "So you don't want to go down that way?" he asked.

"No."

We walked down Terrace Hill Street and then to Main and dropped Linda back home.

Once it was just the two of us walking home, Ivan asked, "Does that big old house remind you of something?"

I nodded.

"The German house in the country?"

I shook my head.

"Are you sure you don't want to go look at it with me?"

"I'm sure."

"That's too bad," said Ivan. "Because it's an interesting place and I thought you'd enjoy seeing it up close."

I shivered at the thought of it.

"It was built in the eighteen hundreds by the man who owned the railroads," he said. "He wanted it to look like — "

I squeezed Ivan's hand so hard that he looked at me and stopped talking mid-sentence.

Chapter Fourteen

Stolen

One Saturday morning, Marusia burst through the front door with a grin on her face and a grocery bag in her arms. I had been at the library all morning and had just gotten home a few moments before.

"You will never guess what happened today," she said, taking off her winter coat.

"You got a new job?"

Marusia's face fell. After harvest finished, she hadn't been able to find another full-time job. Since the beginning of December she had been working four mornings a week at the laundromat that had opened up downtown, but it didn't pay nearly as much as what she had made at the farm.

"Not that." She dug her hand deep into her coat pocket and pulled out three small stubs of paper. "Tickets to the movies — for tonight," she said. "One of my customers gave them to me."

How exciting! I had walked past the movie theatre with Mychailo, but never dreamed that I could ever go. "What movie will we see?"

"*Cinderella* is playing," said Marusia. "It's the English version of *Popelyushka*."

Popelyushka was a fairy tale that tugged at my memory. It seemed that I had known the story for my whole life.

Ivan was working at the church, but as soon as he got in, we told him the good news. We had a quick supper, then we bundled up for our special evening out. It took only a few minutes to get to the theatre. A lineup had formed, but Ivan walked up to a man wearing a red hat and showed him our tickets. He waved us inside.

The first room we stepped into was a huge open area decorated with old-fashioned paintings on the ceiling and red velvet curtains. One wall was plastered with old movie posters. There was a dark-haired woman with red lipstick on the poster for a movie called *Gone With the Wind*. I tugged Ivan's hand and pointed. He grinned. Marusia looked just as pretty this evening, with her hair combed out and her lipstick on.

We walked through the opening in the curtains and into the theatre itself. The seats were filling quickly, but I pointed to the front row. It was nearly empty. We hurried before others noticed, and got the three seats in the exact centre. I snuggled into my chair and leaned way back so I could see the whole giant screen above me. *Cinderella* started like a big book being opened and a voice saying, "Once upon a time in a faraway land there was a tiny kingdom . . ."

I felt like I had stepped inside a story book. Never before had I seen a movie made with drawings instead of people, and never before had I watched a movie in "Technicolor." The movies that Vater took us to were all about

Hitler and how he was a hero. They were very serious and not interesting. *Cinderella* was nothing like that. It had songs and dances and happy things, even though the story was sad in parts. Cinderella's bare bedroom in the big mansion at the beginning of the movie made my stomach flip. Did the bedrooms in Yates Castle look like this?

After the movie was over, the three of us walked home in the dark. Ivan had his arm around Marusia's waist and I walked a few steps ahead of them, my hands shoved into the pockets of my winter coat. As we walked, I thought of the song that Cinderella sang, about a dream being a wish your heart makes. I had never thought of dreams like that before. Was my heart trying to tell me something in my dreams? It didn't seem like a wish to me. It was more like a fear.

✤ ✤ ✤

Marusia and Ivan sat in the kitchen together and chatted when we got home from the movies. I wanted to give them time with each other, so instead of sitting with them, I went up to my bedroom. I sat on my bed and looked at my beautiful room with new appreciation. I had an attic bedroom like Cinderella's, but mine was cosy and warm. The lilac-painted walls made me feel safe and my wooden crate nightstand was simple, but it held my library books and my lamp. What more did I need? How lucky I was to be loved by Marusia and Ivan. I drew out a library book and hugged it to my chest . . .

Dark shadows dance on the scuffed white walls. Someone else's fingernail scratches are etched around the glass doorknob and there are tiny splinters of wood fraying from the door itself. The one window is too high to peer out of so

I grab onto the bars and try to hoist myself up. For a few trembling moments I look out at the dirt-trampled snow far below. My arms give out and I fall back down to the floor. Why am I a prisoner in this house?

My throat is raw from screaming and my fingernails are bloodied from scrabbling at the doorknob. I lie on the wooden floor and stare up at the bare lightbulb. I can hear nothing but my own gasping breaths. Then a thump-thumping of hard shoes just outside my door. Shuffling. A struggle. A child screams down the hallway. A door slams shut.

Another stolen child.

I pray for the door to open. I pray for a way to escape.

Hours or days pass and I hear something at my window. How can this be? I am on the second floor. Have I died and is it an angel tapping there? But then I realize that someone is throwing stones at the window. I get up off the floor and grip the window bars. With my bare feet flat against the wall, I climb up to the window like I'm climbing a mountain. I get my feet onto the ledge and hoist myself up.

A woman. Eyes swollen nearly shut from weeping. Head covered with a faded kerchief. She sees me through the window pane and waves frantically at first, but then realizes that I am not the child she is looking for. How many stolen children are in this place?

"Help me!" I scream. I pound on the window.

A soldier nudges her with his rifle.

From a room down the hallway, I hear a child cry, "Mama!" That child pounds on the window too.

Why can I hear the child scream and pound, but the woman cannot? She turns and scans the windows one last time and the soldier hits her in the face with his rifle, knocking her to her knees.

I hear the door open behind me. A woman dressed in white comes into the room and orders me away from the window, but I stay where I am. "Help!"

The nurse is beside me now and she wraps an arm around my waist. I kick and thrash. I feel a cold sting on my shoulder. Suddenly I feel weak. I cannot hold onto the bars any longer. I fall into the woman's arms.

The library book slipped out of my hand and landed on my toe. I rubbed my eyes and looked around. I was standing in my own lilac bedroom in the house that Ivan built on Sheridan Street in Brantford. It was dark outside but my lamp was on. No bars on the window. The door open. I was safe. My heart felt like it would explode.

I didn't want to be alone, so I got up and walked down the stairs. Marusia and Ivan were no longer in the kitchen drinking tea. I poked my head into their bedroom. Ivan was softly snoring and Marusia was sound asleep. We still had no living room furniture so I sat in the middle of the floor and stared out our front window.

My flashes of the past before this had been short. This one had been terrifyingly long. I struggled to remember more bits about the building . . . A rich person's home in the city that had been transformed into something horrible. Tall white steps leading to an elegant entryway with a vaulted ceiling. Stairs on either side leading up up up. I remembered being carried like a sack of grain up those stairs. Being locked in a room. Others were locked in rooms beside me. What had I done to deserve this punishment? What happened before that

. . . and what happened after? My mind was a blank.

A warm hand rested on my shoulder. It took me a few moments to realize I was back in the present. Marusia was kneeling at my side. "Nadia . . . Nadia . . . Are you all right?"

"I have remembered more."

"Do you want to talk about it?"

I didn't say anything for a few minutes, but instead tried to breathe slowly to calm down my heart. "I dreamt of being locked in a big house."

"The German farmhouse?" Marusia asked.

"No," I said. "This was a fancy house in the city."

Marusia's brow furrowed. "How old were you?"

"I don't know . . . too short to see out the window."

"So this is a memory from before you lived with the Germans . . . " Marusia said, as much to herself as to me.

"*Before* I lived with the Germans? What does that mean?" I asked. I could feel her trembling beside me. I think she was weeping in the darkness but didn't want me to know it.

"I have told you that you are not German," she said. "That was not your birth family."

If that family wasn't my birth family, who were they? And who *was* my birth family?

I knew Marusia and Ivan were not my birth parents, but I knew they loved me. It felt right that the Germans weren't my parents. Mutter never treated me the same as Eva. But how did I get there and who were my *real* parents? None of this made sense.

"Then who am I?"

Marusia shook her head. "I don't know exactly who

you are, but you are Ukrainian. I know that for a fact."

"But — how can you know?"

"Small things that you did without knowing it," she said.

"Like what?" I asked.

"The way you crossed yourself after a prayer," she said. "And you would sing the *kolysanka* to yourself when you thought no one was listening."

"I thought it was my secret song."

"Yes," said Marusia, hugging me. "I know you thought that. You also didn't look like anyone else in that German family."

I nodded in agreement.

"And you spoke German with a Ukrainian accent," she said with a smile.

"I did?"

"Very much so."

It was a jumble in my head, but I was comforted to know that those people weren't my family. Every time a student at school would taunt me, calling me a Hitler girl or Nazi Nadia, I felt a tug of shame. I had met many kind Germans, both in Canada and during the war. I felt sorry for Mutter because she was always sad, but she was not kind to me. And Vater was almost a stranger. A cold, hard stranger. After the war, when I heard about the many evil things that Hitler had done, it made me feel ashamed of who I might be.

And that one big question still hung over me. Who am I?

I didn't want to go back to my room and I was too shaken to be alone. Ivan only had a few more hours to sleep

before it would be time for him to get up for work, so
Marusia tiptoed back to the bedroom and got a blanket
and pillows and we slept on the floor in the middle of the
living room, hugging each other tightly.

I couldn't get to sleep. I didn't want to think about that
house. I thought about Cinderella and how she could
dream about what her heart wished for. As I drifted
towards sleep again, a memory of another mother long
ago appeared in my mind . . .

I sat on her warm lap in the dark with my arms around
her waist and breathed in her faint scent of lilac. I did not
want to let her go. She cooed the *kolysanka* in my ear. A
warm tear splashed on my cheek. I looked up. Despite the
darkness I saw tears on her face . . .

But who was she?

It was nearly time for Christmas holidays and a soft blanket of snow covered the streets and houses. I got out of the
habit of going to Linda's house. We were still friends, but
the thought of being close to Yates Castle made me
uncomfortable. Going to church wasn't the same, either.
The smell of incense no longer gave me comfort.

One day, after school and before Ivan or Marusia got
home, I sat on my swing in the backyard and closed my
eyes and tried very hard just to think of my past. So often,
the memories would come to me unexpectedly. How I
would love to be able to think of them on purpose so
I could sort it all out. I could hear someone banging a
hammer in the distance and the sound reminded me of
mortar fire. Big soft snowflakes hit my head and shoulders. I closed my eyes and held my face to the sky. As each

flake tickled my face, I tried to remember the past.

"Boo!"

I screamed and nearly fell off the swing.

"Hey, I really scared you," Mychailo said. "You should see your face."

"That wasn't very nice," I snapped at him. My heart was still pounding.

"Do you want to go to the park?" he asked.

"It's too cold," I said.

Mychailo rolled his eyes. "If the snow bothers you, why are you sitting out here on the swing getting snowed on?"

"Fine, let's go to the park," I said. Going to the park might be just the thing to clear my head. I wrote a note for Marusia and Ivan and propped it on top of the icebox.

We got to the park, but then Mychailo didn't want to stop because there were some boys from the school horsing around with a toboggan.

"We can just walk around," I told him. "Or maybe go to the library."

We walked past our school, and the library, through Victoria Park and all the way to the market square without saying a word to each other. It wasn't a market day so the square was empty. I gazed into store windows filled with toys and perfumes and other things for Christmas — there was so much choice.

Mychailo finally asked, "What are you thinking about?"

"Nothing," I answered.

"That's not true," he replied. "You've got a sad look on your face. Are you thinking about your old home?"

I looked up at him in surprise. "What do you mean?"

"What I mean is pretty simple," he said. "Don't you

ever think about the home you left behind?"

"It's such a jumble," I told him. "But I do think about it a lot."

Mychailo must have had some similar experiences. He had lived in a camp just like us. He had lived through the war. But this was something that we never talked about. I wasn't sure if it was because it was too painful for him, or if it was because his mind wouldn't let him remember, like what happened to me.

"What do you remember about the war?" I asked him.

"Everything," he said, kicking at a stone with the tip of his shoe. "Sometimes I wish I could forget."

"Can you tell me what you remember?" I asked. "Maybe it will help *me* remember."

"Smells, most of all," he answered. "Gunpowder and rot and blood."

Even as he said the words, my nose wrinkled at the memories.

"The nicest thing about Canada is that they don't have those smells here."

Mychailo was right. In Canada, everything smelled like it had just been washed.

We walked to the library in silence. Mychailo pulled open the heavy side door that led directly to the children's department. As I stepped in I took a deep breath, savouring the scent of furniture polish, soap and books. Much better than the smell of war.

When I got back home, Marusia and Ivan were there, but I felt like being alone. I sat on my swing in the snow and thought about the smells that haunted Mychailo. So much of my past I had started to remember. I willed myself to think about my escape with Marusia, first remembering the parts that came easily to me, and then thinking about what happened next, starting with our last days before reaching the DP camp . . .

The train stopped. We huddled together on the flatcar with many other escapees. Rain poured down but one man took off his frayed greatcoat and tried to cover us all.

A jeep pulled up. Soviet soldiers piled out. There was a fight, gunshots, screams. Marusia gripped my hand as we and the other escapees scattered. We ran. Another gunshot. I felt a bullet whiz past my shoulder. We were the only ones not caught.

We ran and ran. My ribs ached but we kept on going until it was the blackest part of night, and we reached a deserted village. The Soviets had already been here. My nose wrinkled at the familiar stink of blood and smoke. Where once a house had stood, now there was just a hole in the ground — the remains of a root cellar. Marusia stumbled down first and then lifted me in.

I shivered with the cold and the wet — the dirty rag that had once been my pink dress did not keep me warm. How long Marusia and I huddled together in the rubble on the floor of the cellar I did not know. We tried to cover ourselves with leaves. Tried to sleep.

The next morning. I woke with a start when Marusia screamed and rolled on top of me. I could not get my breath, and pushed at her to get her off me, but she wouldn't move. I heard a *whoosh*, then saw a pitchfork. It missed my head by an inch. Standing above us was a woman shrivelled and bent with age. She reached down to grab the handle of the pitchfork, but Marusia swung around and held onto the blades.

"Please don't hurt us," Marusia pleaded in German.

The woman blinked in surprise. "A woman and child!" she murmured. "I thought you were more Russian soldiers."

"We have been running from them," said Marusia.

"Are you Germans?"

"No," said Marusia. "We are foreign workers."

"Why don't you go back with them?" the woman asked, pointing in the direction of the Soviets' advance.

"They're as bad as the Nazis," said Marusia.

"Come on then," said the woman, turning her back on us.

I helped Marusia to her feet. She gripped the handle of the pitchfork and we climbed out of the root cellar.

The old woman assumed our obedience and did not look back. Now that it was light, I could see the charred ruins of cottages lining the street. We followed her to what used to be the village square. All was rubble except for the corner of a church. The burnt wood and glass shards had been shoved to one side of the church floor. Within the protection of where the two remaining walls met, the floor was covered with a filthy bedsheet. On it lay a young woman slashed with blood and bruises. At first I thought she was dead, but then I noticed a slight movement of her face.

"My granddaughter survived," said the old woman. "But just barely. I need you to watch her while I look for food."

We stayed there for several days. The old woman shared with us the food she managed to scrounge. Marusia cleaned the granddaughter's wounds and disinfected them with a tincture she made from leaves and stalks. When we left, the old woman pointed us in the direction of the nearest Displaced Person's camp . . .

That night I dreamed the scent of manure and gunpowder, blood and dirt. And lilacs.

Chapter Fifteen

Inspector Sutton

"Students, look smart," Miss Ferris said the next morning. "We're having a visitor after recess and I want you all to be on your best behaviour."

I looked over to Linda. She arched an eyebrow. When Miss Ferris turned to write something on the blackboard, Linda leaned towards my desk and whispered, "It's probably the inspector."

I didn't know what that meant. I noticed that many of the students seemed on edge and Miss Ferris herself spoke with a voice that seemed half-strangled. Whoever this inspector was, I didn't look forward to seeing him.

I finally got my chance to ask Linda about the visitor once the recess bell rang. "They send a boss a couple of times every year," she explained. "If a teacher isn't doing a good job, she can get fired."

"What about the students?" I asked.

"An inspector can cause trouble for students too," said Linda. "If you're late for school a lot or if you're absent too many times, the inspector wants to see you. I dread it when they come."

I thought of my horrible first day of school and how I had left the yard without permission. "Do you think I'll be in trouble because of leaving school on the first day?" I asked.

She paused to consider. "If you were going to get into trouble, it would have happened by now. That was months ago."

Her words made me feel slightly less frightened about the inspector's visit, but like everyone else, I was not looking forward to it.

As we were lining up to go back into school after the recess bell rang, a black taxi pulled up. All I could see through the back window was the head and shoulders of a woman.

I nudged Linda with my elbow and whispered, "Is that the inspector?"

Linda looked doubtful. "I've never seen a lady inspector."

Miss Ferris came out and made us step smartly in line. We marched into our class and took our seats. She rapped a ruler on her desk to get our attention.

"Inspector Sutton is here," she said, a look of panic on her face. "When she comes in, I shall clap my hands twice and you will say, in unison, 'Good morning, Inspector Sutton.'"

Just then the door flew open and an unsmiling woman carrying a black satchel strode in. Her grey hair was pulled into a loose bun at the nape of her neck and she wore a brown tailored suit over a white men's style shirt. When I had seen her in the taxi, I was nervous, but now seeing her in front of me, I was terrified. It wasn't a normal kind of terror. Something deep inside told me that this woman was going to harm me. I had a panicked urge to bolt from the classroom, but the inspector was standing in front of the only exit. It was all I could do to stay seated. I gripped the sides of my desk to keep from shaking.

Miss Ferris was also nervous. Was she feeling the same as me? Her face was drained of colour. She forgot to clap her hands, so some students jumped out of their seats, but not everyone. I was the last to get to my feet. A few straggling voices called out, "Good morning, Inspector Sutton."

The inspector put her satchel on the floor and her hands on her hips. "Is that the best you can do?"

"GOOD MORNING, INSPECTOR SUTTON!" we shouted out in unison.

"Good morning class," she said. Then, using her hands like the conductor of an orchestra, she motioned for us to sit down.

"Now, Miss Ferris." The inspector turned away from us and gazed upon our teacher. "What poem can your students recite for me?"

"Um . . . Miss . . . Inspector Sutton . . . we haven't practised recitations recently." Miss Ferris clutched her ruler as if it were a lifeline.

"Can they sing a song for me?"

Miss Ferris brightened. "They can sing 'The Maple Leaf Forever.'"

"Very good," said Inspector Sutton. "Let's hear it."

Miss Ferris got us all to stand up again and we sang the song. Most of us seemed to be on key and we kept fairly good time with each other, I thought. Miss Ferris looked expectantly at Miss Sutton.

"Good," said the inspector.

She walked behind Miss Ferris's desk and grabbed the back of her chair, dragged it across the floor and positioned it to face us, then she sat down. "That's better," she said. She drew a pair of wire-rimmed spectacles out of her suit pocket and perched them on the end of her nose. She took a black notebook out of her satchel, then pointed to one student at a time. Each was made to stand and answer a single question and then sit down. She jotted down notes about each of us. They weren't difficult questions, but it was terrifying nonetheless. My question was, "What is your favourite colour?" When I told her it was lilac, she smiled and said that my English was good for a newcomer.

After she was finished, Inspector Sutton put Miss Ferris's chair back behind the desk and walked to the door. I was so relieved that she was leaving. She hadn't said anything about me running away from school on that first day. Linda had been right.

I was almost starting to breathe again when the inspector paused. It was like she had just remembered something. She opened her satchel and took out the black notebook, flipping through the pages with a frown on her face. "The new girl . . . Nadia?" She looked over her spectacles and surveyed the class yet again.

I stood up.

"Come here," she said with a smile. "You can carry my bag."

The thought of going near that woman made me feel like I was going to be sick to my stomach. I took one deep calming breath and began to walk over to her. She smelled like mothballs.

Her bag was surprisingly heavy and I needed both hands to carry it. She walked out of the room and I stumbled after her. She was waiting at the door to the grade one class when I caught up with her.

"Thank you," she said. "That bag gets so heavy to carry around all day. Here's a little something for your trouble."

She pulled a cello-wrapped hard candy from her pocket and held it out to me.

I stared at that candy on her outstretched palm. Without knowing why I was doing it or where I was going, I bolted down the hallway. All I knew was that I had to get away. I pushed open the outside door and kept on running. It was cold and I was without my winter coat and boots but that didn't stop me. The chill against my face felt like freedom.

"Nadia, come back!" Inspector Sutton called.

I didn't stop running, but turned to look. She was standing in the entranceway with a look of shock on her face. I was grateful that she wasn't following me. When I turned a moment later, to check, she was gone.

I didn't know where I was going, but a feeling deep inside me told me that my life depended on getting away from that brown-suited woman. I didn't want to go home. Wouldn't that be the first place she would look for me?

My legs took me on my usual route to the library. I hid behind a snowbank when I heard a car. I could see the children's entrance, but there was a group of mothers with little children in strollers chatting in front of it. I ran up the steps to the main doors, painfully aware that I was in full view of anyone passing by. Luckily, none of the chatting mothers noticed me. When I got to the top, I opened the door just a crack. My face was blasted with warm air as I peered in. No one was there, so I stepped inside. I didn't realize how chilled to the bone I was until the warmth of the inside air wrapped around me. I could hear voices coming out of the main library room, so I slipped down the steps to the children's department.

It was story time in the picture-book room, but the novel room looked empty. I sat on the floor in the corner farthest from the door and wrapped my arms around my legs and rocked my body back and forth, chanting the *kolysanka*. My whole body trembled — not just from being out in the cold, but from my memories. Images of a brown-suited woman invaded my mind. I tried to think of other things but it was no use. I was frightened beyond words.

Chapter Sixteen

Brown Sisters

I shiver at the foot of our bed, my arms wrapping around my knees for warmth. We layer our clothing, but the cold always seeps through. We have one threadbare wool blanket that is too worthless to barter for food. I tuck it lovingly around my baba, *but her lips are still blue. Lida walks into the bedroom holding a chipped bowl in her hands. It contains what we like to call soup, but we both know there is little nourishment in it: water, faint flavour from bones boiled dozens of times, scraps of potato or cabbage, and anything else we can find to put in it.*

She sets the bowl down on the nightstand and props up Baba's head and shoulders with a pillow. Baba's eyes flicker open. She looks at me and then at Lida. "My granddaughters," she says. "Don't waste this food on me. I am not long for this world."

Lida and I both know what Baba says is true, but how can we not try to save her? She is all the family we have left. Tato was taken by the Soviet police in early summer, like so many of the other Ukrainian men. Weeks after that, Mama was taken by the Nazi police. Old people and children

*don't get ration cards. Baba's hoarded bits got us through
the fall. But now that it is the dead of winter, we are desperate. We have burned most of our furniture for warmth
and bartered our precious books. Even our beloved lilac
bush has been hacked to pieces and burnt as firewood.*

*Lida leans on the edge of the bed and offers a spoonful
of soup, but Baba refuses to open her lips. Lida sighs.
"What if we share?"*

Baba nods. "You eat first."

*We pass the spoon around, sharing the watery soup one
sip at a time.*

*Once Baba falls back to sleep, we go out to the street to
beg. First we sit in front of the bakery. When Sarah and her
parents were alive, they would always find something for us
— even if it was just a stale bun. But they were among the
first that the Nazis took.*

*The woman who comes out now speaks German. She
pushes us away with a broom. We sit on the steps in front
of the boarded-up church, huddling close together for
warmth. I remember a time when we could go inside.
Mama and Tato were still with us. The smell of incense
made me feel safe. But people don't come here anymore.
Besides, there are too many beggars and not enough food.
We are given not even a crust of bread.*

*I notice that a snaking lineup of children has suddenly
formed outside the gates of what used to be the synagogue.
Whenever a line forms, we know to run to it. Does it matter
what is being given out? It will be better than nothing.*

*When we get closer we see two women dressed in brown
suits with white collars and cuffs. "Maybe they're nuns," I
say hopefully.*

Lida looks at me with surprise. "The Nazis got rid of the sisters long ago."

One of the women writes notes in a black leather book. The other dips her hand into a large paper bag and brings out candies. My stomach rumbles at the sight. I cannot remember the last time I have eaten anything other than maggoty bread or watery soup.

I stand on my tiptoes and see that Sofia from down the street is talking to the brown sisters now. She does a little whoop for joy when she gets candy. Finally it is my turn. Lida stands behind me, her hands resting on my shoulders.

"What lovely blond hair you have," the woman says to me in German. She crouches down until her face is level with mine. "And blue eyes."

I smile politely. My blond hair often helps when begging from Germans.

"Girls, are you sisters?" the woman taking notes asks.

"Yes," I say.

"Where do you live?" she asks.

"In that house." I point to our whitewashed cottage at the end of the street.

"Is she telling the truth?" the woman asks Lida with a smile.

"Yes."

The other woman reaches into her bag and draws out three candies. She gives all of them to me. The look of hope on Lida's face crumbles. The woman reaches back into the bag and draws out three more sweets. She holds them just under Lida's nose. "Tell me how old you are and how old your little sister is."

"Larissa is five," Lida says. "And I am eight."

The woman grins. She puts the three candies into Lida's palm.

Lida grabs my hand and we run back home, giggling. Baba is asleep when we get there. Lida and I each put one of our candies on her nightstand, and then we sit together, leaning against our cold hearth, and savour our candies.

The three of us sleep together in the big bed for warmth. Usually Baba hugs us tight and sings the kolysanka. *But since she is already asleep, Lida and I sing it softly to ourselves.*

When I first hear the banging, I think it is a dream. I know it is real when Baba sits up in bed and wraps her bony arms around us. "Do not open the door," she hisses.

The three of us sit in the dark, clinging to each other and praying that whoever is on the other side will go away. But the banging continues. The door bursts open. A beam of light darts through the main room, then finds the bedroom. The doorway fills with the silhouette of two soldiers; one holding a flashlight and the other pointing a rifle at us. When my eyes get used to the brightness, I see a third person — the woman in brown who gave us candy.

She comes to the bed and grabs me roughly by the arm, but Baba won't let go. The woman turns to the soldiers. "Take her."

Baba holds on with such strength that I have bruises on my ribcage for days after, but in the end she is no match for two armed men. One throws me over his shoulder. The other does the same with Lida.

"Baba!" I scream as they carry us out the door.

Baba falls back on the bed amid torn bedclothes, a trickle of blood on her cheek. Her arms extend towards us and the look on her face makes my heart crumble. Just before the flashlight clicks off, I notice the two candies sitting at her nightstand. Untouched.

Lida and I are thrown into the back of a truck. It smells like urine. Other children are weeping. Lida and I find each other in the darkness and clutch each other in fear and desperation.

I felt a hand on my shoulder. Then a voice came.

"Nadia, are you okay?" Miss Barry.

I rubbed my eyes, blinked twice and looked around me. I was crouched in the corner of the novel room in the children's department of the public library. In Brantford. I was safe. That girl was my sister. Lida. Where is she now?

I am not Nadia. I am not Gretchen. My name is Larissa!

I felt something warm cover my back and shoulders. "You're shivering," said Miss Barry. "Where is your coat?"

I looked at her but didn't answer. My mind was still filled with images from the past.

"Let's get you into the staff room," she said. "There's a sofa for you to lie down on."

She gently picked me up and carried me into the other room. "I am going to get in touch with your parents." I watched as her lips continued to move, but I didn't understand anything more that she said. My mind had returned to the past . . .

I am in a large white room with bright lights. Maybe a hospital room, but the children are frightened, not sick. When it is my turn, the nurse makes me remove everything but my underwear. My face is hot with shame. I scream when she holds a metal instrument up to my face. "Tsk tsk," she says, then in German, "This is a caliper — for measuring. Nothing to be afraid of."

Her words do not comfort me. As she measures and takes notes, a different woman takes photographs of me — from the front, the side, the back.

What are they doing? What does this mean?

My nose is measured in three places. "Turn around," she says. I feel the cold metal prongs dig into the sides of my head. She writes more numbers in her book. She measures my legs and my arms and waist. Throughout all of this, I stand there, too frightened to move.

When she is finished, she grips my left hand palm upward and I watch in fear as she carefully injects pinpricks of black into my wrist. Is this poison? When she's finished, I hold it up to my face. It looks like a tiny mole.

She grabs my hair roughly and I feel a pinprick behind my ear. "There," she says. "You are a Lebensborn."

What is a Lebensborn? *I know of the children who disappear. One day they are begging on the street and the next day it's as if they never existed. Are they* Lebensborn *too?*

Lida's turn is next. She is measured and photographed, but isn't marked with black.

When all the children are measured, we are sorted into two groups: those with black marks and those without. I am in one. Lida is in the other. Her group is marched to the door.

"Please!" I scream. "Let me go with my sister!"

"You are the lucky one," says the woman in white.

"Lida!" I scream.

Lida turns and looks. Her eyes are filled with despair. She is shoved out the door. I try to run after her but they hold me back.

Days blur. Children marching. Children saluting the führer. *We are given small rations of plain food. At first I gobble it down, but then I feel guilty that I can't save some to give to Baba or Lida. The thought of eating this food makes me feel ill. I speak Ukrainian to one of the other children, but a woman in white slaps my face. "You are German!" she says. "Speak German."*

The next time I speak my own language, I am dragged away. They kick me down a flight of wooden stairs and I land on the dirt floor. It is dark and all I can see are the glowing eyes of rats. I clasp my arms around my knees and try to stay warm. When the women in white come to get me, the brightness from outside almost blinds me.

I take classes with the other children. A woman who does not smile teaches us the rules we are to live by. Ukrainians and Poles are sub-human. Those who are allowed to live will be slaves to the Aryans. "You are Aryans," she tells us. "The people you think were your parents are thieves. They stole you from your Aryan parents and now we will give you back."

I know she speaks lies.

"Jews are rats," she continues. "None deserve to live."

I think of Sarah and her parents. They were Jewish and they were taken away. Sarah's mother had always found me bread. Sarah's father never hurt a soul.

"You are wrong!" I cry.

I cover my mouth, but it is too late.

The other students regard me with round-eyed horror.

I am put in a truck and taken away from the other children. A soldier throws me over his shoulder and carries me up a tall set of white steps and into a mansion. I pound on his back and scream for my baba. I am locked into a bare white room and given no food or water. I pound on the door but no one comes. The next day I call in German. Someone brings water . . .

I was suddenly aware of the blanket that was draped over my shoulders. It had the faint scent of lavender and talcum powder. I snuggled into it, thankful for its warmth. The rush of memory faded and I looked around me. I was lying on a sofa in a room near Miss Barry's desk. She sat on a stool in front of me, her hands gripped around a glass of water. All at once, the image of the school inspector filled my mind. "Please don't send me back to school!"

"You're safe with me," said Miss Barry. "I phoned your father at the foundry. He asked me to sit with you until he can get here."

She held the glass of water out to me. I took grateful sips. My mouth felt like sawdust. I closed my eyes.

Chapter Seventeen

Gretchen

Gretchen Himmel. With a flash of understanding, I remembered *becoming* Gretchen Himmel.

At first I only pretended to believe that I was German. But the more I lied, the more real it became. I first spoke German to make the punishment stop, but soon I was thinking in German. Marching with the other children, reciting long poems and songs about Hitler and the Reich. We were born to rule the world. I was proud to be one of the chosen.

Larissa disappeared and Gretchen emerged . . .

Gretchen knows that the woman I called Baba was not my grandmother. She stole me from my parents, who are decent German farmers. The man who called me daughter was a bandit. The woman I called mother was a spy. That girl is not my sister. She is an evil slave and she was trying to trick me. She is being punished for her crimes. Jews are rats. They deserve to die. I can hardly wait to go back home, to my real parents. My name is Gretchen. I've seen my birth certificate and it says Gretchen Himmel. *It is a relief to leave the confusion behind.*

I am bathed, then dressed in a crisp white blouse and blue tunic and shoes that pinch at the heel. My hair is clean and combed and braided. I sit by myself in the back seat of a long black car and breathe in the clean scent of freshly polished leather. The car stops at a huge farmhouse in the country. The fields around it go on for miles and are tended by slaves. The driver is a soldier in a dove grey uniform and he opens the door for me with a smile. He says, "I am sure you are glad to be home, Gretchen."

I step out of the car and gulp in the country air. A blond girl in a pale pink dress pushes open the door of the house and runs to me. A sad-eyed blond woman follows close behind.

"My big sister has finally arrived!" the little girl says.

Before I know it, she has wrapped her arms around my waist. She is crying or laughing, I don't know which. "I am so glad you're home," says Eva in German.

Is this my home? I don't remember it. But I don't remember many things. I am relieved to be safe, in a place called home.

Eva tugs me by the hand, pulling me to the open door of the big farmhouse. The blond woman walks a few steps behind us. She has barely greeted me, but Eva tells me she's our mutti. *I watch her through the corner of my eye and see that she's wiping a tear away from her cheek.*

The door of the house opens up to a big entryway that smells of bleach. My heart pounds, but Eva squeezes my hand.

She leads me into a room just beyond the entryway and I gasp. Two walls are lined from floor to ceiling with books, most in German, but some in other languages too. I hunger to touch them. The books call to me. Above the fireplace is a huge portrait of Hitler, our leader and saviour. On the mantel is a framed picture of a sad-looking young man in a dark uniform.

"That's our Geert," says Eva.

"He is very handsome," I say.

The woman who is supposed to be our mother stands behind us and regards the photo. I can hear her sniffle. "Your brother was handsome," she says. "And brave. He died while fighting for the Fatherland."

She leaves the room and Eva and I are alone. "Mutti has been so sad since Geert died. Maybe she'll cheer up now that you've come."

I don't remember Geert, and now he's gone. That makes me feel guilty. "I am sad that our brother died too."

Eva looks at me strangely, then blinks. "You'll like it here," she says. "There's lots of food."

"Your father is on his way," said Miss Barry.

I blinked once, slowly, and looked around. I was on the sofa in the staff room at the library. I looked down and saw that I was holding a glass of water. I took a sip. Miss Barry brushed a wisp of hair out of my eyes. It was such a gentle gesture that I almost wept . . .

Eva is right. There is a lot of food. Apples and mushrooms and noodles and sauce, meat and stuffing. Mutter places it all on the dining room table. But whatever I put in my mouth sits like a lump of coal on my tongue. Mutter makes chocolate cake with icing to entice me. She makes biscuits in the shape of men and draws on a face in white icing. Eva loves it all and gulps down every bit. I force myself to eat even when it makes me feel ill.

I want the hurt to go away from Mutter's eyes.

I have my own room with a giant four-poster bed, but I cannot sleep. Dark uniformed men dine at our table and talk together until the wee hours of the morning. I hear clinking of glasses and roars of laughter. I rarely see Vater except at these meetings. Eva and I put on our prettiest dresses and go downstairs to greet the guests. Vater introduces us as his "two flowers for the Fatherland."

When I am finally able to go back to my room, I sing a song of nonsense words to block out the noises, but I cannot sleep.

✦ ✦ ✦

In spring the OST woman arrives at the farm in the truck. She smells bad and I do not like her, but the next time I see her she no longer wears the OST badge and she is clean. Mutter tells us to call her Cook. Eva and I play outside together. We collect lilacs to give to Mutter. She puts them in a vase and sets them in the middle of the kitchen table. She says Cook will like them. Mutter prefers bought ones for the dining room.

We are not allowed to go into the fields where the slaves are. I see a slave come to the door. Cook bandages its wound. Mutter doesn't see that. Neither does Eva. I should tell Mutter about it, but for some reason, I don't.

Mutter begins to take Eva on errands but leaves me at home. When they are gone, I open up the book room and breathe in the scent of old paper. It makes my heart ache to smell it, but somehow it makes me happy too. I climb up on the desk and draw out a book with gold lettering on the spine. The one beside it crashes to the ground, bending the pages.

My heart pounds when I hear footsteps. It is only Cook. She picks up the book and puts it back on the shelf. She takes the one I am holding and puts it away too. She examines the books. Her eyes light up and she takes one down and hands it to me.

"You can look at this storybook until they come home," she says.

The title is not in German. "Popelyushka!" I say. Cook smiles.

❖ ❖ ❖

Another time, I sit under the lilac bushes and whisper my nonsense song under my breath. Cook comes up to me. I notice that her hands are red with work and her eyes look tired and sad. I feel sorry for her even though she is an animal. I say in German, "Would you like to hear me sing?"

She nods.

I sing again my secret song. Cook weeps. On the second verse, with a tear-filled voice, she joins in. She sings the entire song with me.

How can she know my secret language? "You know my kolysanka," I say. She tries to hug me but I push her away. Mutter has told me to stay away from the slaves.

Cook swallows back her tears, and then in harsh, precise German she says, "This is not your home."

I am shocked speechless.

But she isn't finished. There is more. "I will protect you."

The harsh ringing of a telephone jarred me back to the present. I blinked and looked around. The past was so real, yet here I was, lying on a sofa in the staff room of the library. I could hear Miss Barry's voice, talking to someone on the other end of the telephone. Then her voice faded . . .

When Mutter and Eva come back from their errands, I am bursting to tell them what Cook said. She should be punished for her crime. But for some reason I say nothing. The next time Eva and Mutter go away, Cook invites me to share a meal in the kitchen with her. It is slave food — a thin soup with black bread. I take one spoonful of the thin broth and begin to weep. I try to remember what the soup reminds me of, but my memory has been washed clean.

We are to go to a rally and Mutter has told me to be ready for when they get back. I put on my pink dress and Cook braids my hair. I wait. And wait. And wait.

I walk through the house and see that drawers have been left open and belongings are scattered on the floor. I feel the ground tremble.

"The Soviets are coming," whispers Cook. "We must leave this place."

I do not want to go. This is my home. The room of books is here. The lilac tree is here. Mutter told me to wait. Cook picks me up and carries me out the door. I scream and pull her hair. She drops me on the ground and I fall hard on my back. "Come with me if you want to live," she says. And she begins to walk away.

I follow her, begging her to wait up. I run after her through the fields and I see that the slaves are all gone. When I mention this, Cook turns on me, her face red with fury. "Slavs," she says, "Not slaves. Those people are Ukrainian. They're just like you."

I don't believe her, but this is not the time to argue. She tells me her name is Marusia, not Cook.

We hide behind bushes as Soviet soldiers comb the fields, rooting out the other Slavs — the other stolen people. We are to be brought back to the Soviet Union and punished for letting ourselves be stolen by the Germans.

We walk through forests and countryside studded with landmines. We see villages burning and hear bombs exploding. I do not expect to live.

We join a group of ragged survivors. "Your name is Nadia now," Marusia tells me. "You will never be Gretchen again."

"But why Nadia?" I ask her.

"The name means hope," she says. "It was the middle name of my little sister. She was stolen by the Nazis too."

Chapter Eighteen

Larissa

"Nadia . . . *Nadia*. You arc safe."

The scent of apples and laundry soap. It has to be Marusia. I open my eyes. It is Marusia, in her work clothes. I blink and look around, trying to get my bearings. I am still in the library staff room, bundled up in Miss Barry's blanket. A shiver runs deep in my bones. I am unbearably sad and so very cold.

I feel Marusia's arm around my waist.

Ivan is sitting cross-legged on the carpet, his brow creased with concern. There is no one else here, just me, Marusia and Ivan.

How much trouble was I in for running away from school a second time? Ivan seemed to know what was on my mind. "We told the inspector that you were ill," he said.

I could feel my throat filling with tears — of relief, but also guilt. How long had I been here?

"What time is it?" I asked.

"It's after six," said Ivan. "We have been sitting here with you for hours."

Money was so scarce for us, and I had made them miss work.

I had no control over it — the tears flowed. "I am so sorry," I said. "I didn't mean to cause so much trouble."

"You are not trouble," said Ivan.

Marusia said nothing. I could tell by her gulps of air that she was weeping. I realized it wasn't just me she was weeping about. She had lost another Nadia — her own sister — years ago. Just as I had lost my family. She held me tight and rested her head on my shoulder. I hugged her back. Ivan leaned forward and wrapped his arms around both of us. We wept together.

I don't know how long we stayed like that, but I was suddenly aware that we were still in the library.

"Can we go home?" I asked.

We untangled our arms, but when I tried to get up my joints were so weak that my knees buckled. Marusia was wobbly too.

"Let's get my girls home," said Ivan. He took the blanket off my shoulders and held my coat open so I could slip it on. He must have gone to the school to get it. He wrapped one arm around my waist and another around Marusia's, giving us each support.

When we got home, Marusia warmed up some home-made soup and sliced a few pieces of rye bread. Before, a meal like this would have caused confusing memories and nightmares. But now that my memory was back — parts of it, at least — I was able to think of that last bowl of soup I had shared with my grandmother and sister. It was a sad time, but also a cherished one. How I missed them both.

I still had not pieced together all the details of my life before my parents disappeared. The ache of their loss was like a wound in my heart. I must have been very young when they were taken away. And I realized now that they weren't just taken away. They were dead. Tato was killed by the Soviets and Mama was killed by the Nazis. My teeth chattered — not from the cold but from the realization of all that I had lost.

I wrapped my arms around my chest and rocked back and forth in my chair. Back and forth, back and forth, trying to remember the last time my parents had held me.

But I also knew that Mama and Tato had loved me. Flecks and shadows of scenes from the past told me that. When I thought hard now about Tato, I could remember his warm smile and the last time he tucked me into bed . . . Mama, dear Mama. Her lilting voice as she sang the *kolysanka*.

And Baba? What strength she had. But she couldn't have survived the shock of losing me and Lida.

Lida.

The dark-haired girl in my dream who tried to grab my hand . . . The OST girl in the bombed factory who met my gaze. That was Lida. I knew it now.

Marusia brushed her fingertips lightly on my forearm. "Are you ready to tell us about it?"

I was. At least, about as much as I remembered. It was a relief to say the details out loud.

At first it was all jumbled, but as I continued, my memories began to fall more and more into place. I sorted through the parts of my life when I was Gretchen, and the earlier parts when I was myself. It was a weight taken from my shoulders to know for sure that Vater and Mutter were not my real parents. The thought of Vater in particular made bile rise in my throat. I had a twinge of worry about Eva though. She wasn't my sister, but she was just a child. Where was she now? Was she safe? Did she ever think of me?

Marusia nodded as I spoke. She knew my history from when we met at the farm. Of my earlier life, she had guessed some of it. Ivan must have heard from Marusia all that she knew, but still he sat spellbound.

"I always wondered what your real name was," said Marusia. "Larissa is a beautiful name. And you have a sister named Lida."

"Yes."

My sister. My dear big sister Lida. I started to cry again. "Do you think she still might be alive?" I managed to ask.

"With the memories that you've pieced together, maybe we will be able to find what became of her," said Marusia.

"We'll write to the Red Cross," said Ivan. "We can always hope."

Author's Note

I first heard about the Lebensborn *program from my mother-in-law, the late Lidia (Krawchuk) Skrypuch. The Nazi front passed through her city of Zolochiv twice and soldiers took over her house. She and her parents became prisoners in their own home. One day she overheard bits of conversation from the Nazi officers. Something was happening at her school the next day. Her parents kept her home. When she did go back to school, all of her blond and blue-eyed female classmates had disappeared. She heard they had been taken for the* Lebensborn *program. I asked her what that meant.*

The Lebensborn Program

The Nazi murder of six million Jews during WWII — the Holocaust — is well documented. Most people are not aware of the Nazis' plans for other people. Hitler and the Nazis believed that the Germanic peoples of Central Europe were the descendants of "Aryans" — members of a "master race" whose destiny was to rule the world. Other ethnic groups were sorted into a pecking order, based on how much "Aryan blood" they supposedly had. Most of the peoples of Northern Europe, Great Britain and the Low Countries, as well as parts of France, were considered mostly or partly Aryan. Other groups, especially in the south of Europe, were judged less pure, but acceptable as neighbours and allies. At the very bottom of this hierarchy were the Jews, along with the Roma (Gypsies). The Nazi goal was to exterminate every Jew and Rom in the world. The Nazis also planned to kill people they deemed mentally or physically unfit.

Nazi policy regarding the Slavs — who include the Russians, Ukrainians and Byelorussians, as well as the Poles, Czechs and many others — was less consistent. Slavs were categorized as racially inferior, and Hitler declared that most of their lands in Eastern Europe belonged to Germany as *Lebensraum* ("living space") for the expansion of the Aryan race. Although the Nazis did not call for a Holocaust-style eradication of the Slavs, they treated civilians in Eastern Europe far more harshly than they did civilians elsewhere in Europe. Historians estimate that at least 10 million civilian Slavs were killed by the Germans in Poland and the USSR.

In order to free up "living space" for Aryans, Slavs were to be deported en masse from their homelands. Others were to be sent to Germany as slave labourers. People from the eastern part of Ukraine made up the bulk of these slave labourers. British intelligence reports indicate that the rate of deportation from Soviet Ukraine at times approached 15,000 to 20,000 a day. Soviet cities were full of what the Nazis considered "superfluous eaters" — and death by starvation was common.

Hitler wanted more Aryans to be born, but German women weren't having babies quickly enough. In 1936, Hitler's secret police, the SS, created the *Lebensborn* (Fount of Life) program to increase the number of Aryan children, so that the master race could populate more of Europe. In the beginning, the *Lebensborn* program concentrated on making sure more Aryan babies were produced in Nazi-occupied parts of Europe. But between 1940 and 1942, the Germans also turned their attention to the blond, blue-eyed Polish and Ukrainian children from Eastern Europe, children who also looked Aryan. They began to steal these children from their parents.

There were two methods of rounding up children. The first was to take every child of a certain age in random villages or towns and sort through them, sending some to be killed, assigning others for slave labour and yet others for adoption by Nazi families.

Method two involved using specially trained Nazi women known as Brown Sisters to go through a town searching for children with Aryan features. An Aryan-looking child would be offered candy, giving the Brown Sister the chance to ask questions. The child's home would then be raided in the middle of the night and the child taken away.

The stolen children were put through tests, including the measurement of sixty-two body parts, to ensure that they were "racially valuable." Any tiny shortcoming meant the difference between an adoptive home and either a concentration camp or a slave labour camp.

The final round of racially valuable children was then sent to special homes where the children were brainwashed into thinking that they were German. Some were told that their parents were dead, or had only been spies and liars. Children who were still young — under the age of eight — were then placed with their new Nazi families. Older children were put in Nazi Youth boarding schools or fostered out.

The Nazis went to great lengths to destroy the records of these children when it became clear that Germany would lose the war, so it is hard to know exactly how many were stolen in this way, although it is estimated to be about 250,000 Polish and Ukrainian children alone. The Nazis were so successful with this program that after the war, most of the stolen children refused to leave their German parents, even if their birth parents were still alive and could be located.

The *Ostarbeiters*

The Nazis didn't just steal children. They also forced millions of young adults into forced labour. Those from Eastern Europe were called *Ostarbeiters* (Eastern Workers). They were treated harshly — often worked to death. They were required to wear a badge stitched with the letters *OST* and most lived behind barbed wire in guarded camps. There were 3 to 5.5 million *Ostarbeiters* in Nazi Germany. Most were Ukrainian. Many were forced to work in German munitions factories because the Nazis realized that these factories were prime targets for bombing by the Allied nations. Many *Ostarbeiters* died in Allied bombing raids.

Ukrainian Identity

Before World War II, the land where Ukrainians had lived for more than a thousand years had become part of Poland and the Soviet Union. Since wartime statistics identified people by their citizenship, not ethnicity, Ukrainians were identified as Polish or "Soviet" (which was often inaccurately presumed to be Russian). The fall of the Soviet Union in 1991 has made long-suppressed archival information more available to researchers, and has also heightened public awareness of ethnic distinctions among the peoples of Eastern Europe and the former Soviet Union. Both developments have allowed a truer picture of the Ukrainian experience of World War II to emerge. The nation of Ukraine declared its independence in 1991.